Thin Line Between
Death and Dishonor

Amir Sanchez

www.urbanbooks.net

Urban Books, LLC
300 Farmingdale Road, NY-Route 109
Farmingdale, NY 11735

Thin Line Between Death and Dishonor

ISBN 13: 978-1-60162-563-2
ISBN 10: 1-60162-563-4

First Trade Paperback Printing October 2017
Printed in the United States of America

10 9 8 7 6 5 4 3 2 1

This is a work of fiction. Any references or similarities to actual events, real people, living or dead, or to real locales are intended to give the novel a sense of reality. Any similarity in other names, characters, places, and incidents is entirely coincidental.

Distributed by Kensington Publishing Corp.
Submit orders to:
Customer Service
400 Hahn Road
Westminster, MD 21157-4627
Phone: 1-800-733-3000
Fax: 1-800-659-2436

Thin Line Between
Death and Dishonor

Thin Line Between
Death and Dishonor

by

Amir Sanchez

Acknowledgments

First in order, all praise is to Allah for taking the evil and negative thoughts out of my heart and mind, replacing them with things and talents that will certainly be beneficial in my living a decent, successful life. . . .

All my positive achievements are dedicated to my little cousin, Koran Santana. "Gone but not forgotten, cousin . . . I still feel you." Real niggas die once, while cowards die a million deaths. I wish you could see these niggas now. Those cowards knew they would have never succeeded in their plots had I been around. That is why they waited until I wasn't around. I love you, baby boy. Until we meet again, I'm doing me.

Shout-Outs

To my favorite lady, my mother, Connie Santana, my big sis, Aisha, li'l sisters, Amber, Alaynia, and Arielle, li'l brothers, Rob, Manny, Avery, Mike, Austen, my children, little Amir and Matthew, and my baby girl, Khalena. I love all of y'all. Thank you for your everlasting support. To my aunts, Lisa, Carmen, Barbra, and Michelle, I love y'all too. Love you, Grandmom. Nephews, nieces . . . Unc doing it big!

Special shout-outs to my editor, Jill Serrano, and her nigga, my man, Fly Stunna. My nigga Tuff, Shahir, Migitpimp, Deli, Tim, Buddah Bless, Ceese, Haddi, Lil Da, Omar (Maybache), Sparks, K-Ream, Ms. D. Shields, your vision was crazy . . . Ms. Stevens, wow! Pumkin, Dasha, I should but won't forget y'all . . . Philly, stand up! If you weren't mentioned, that means you aren't part of my movement so stay out of my way! I promise to take this book game to a level where no one has ever taken it. The pen game is vicious.

Prologue

Sunday dinners at the Santana home were always considered sacred. If you wasn't "family," you wasn't permitted to sit down at their table and feast upon the food and fruits of their extravagant labors. The Santana twins, Connie and Consuela, had grown up doing this with their parents and now that they had children of their own, they were proud to carry it on. Every Sunday, the sisters would wake up early and go straight into the kitchen to get started on the food. Connie would season, then marinate the chicken and the *pernil* (Spanish pork shoulder) for a few hours before putting it in the oven to slow cook it. The end result was her delicious fall-off-the-bone baked chicken and roasted pernil. Her sister Consuela was always in charge of the sides. Every Sunday, she would switch it up between rice and beans with homemade potato salad or a baked macaroni and cheese with collard greens and sweet yams. Having grown up in Philly, the girls had learned how to cook all kinds of things from Spanish cuisine to good old down-South comfort food.

"Girl, you put your foot in this one," Connie complimented her sister as she took a big bite out of her corn bread.

"Girl, you know how I get down. A bitch can cook," Consuela laughed.

"Yeah, Mami. This shit is off the chain." Gus, Connie's thirteen-year-old son, invited himself in on the conversation.

"Boy, how many times have I told you not to curse around me and your aunt? I ain't about to be disrespected by my son in my own motherfuckin' house," Connie snapped.

"Dag, Ma, it's not that serious. I was just paying you a compliment," Gus said as he kissed his teeth. Consuela stood up quickly from where she was sitting and yoked her nephew up and got in his face.

"You listen to me, and you listen to me well," she said through clenched teeth. "Don't you ever think you can speak to me or your mother like that. We have fucked people up for thinking they can talk to us any way they want. Don't think just because you're blood you gonna get away with shit like that." Consuela released her nephew from her grip, and he fell back in his chair.

"And that goes for you too, Ka'Leaf and Sha'Ron." Consuela pointed at her own two sons that had silently watched the entire thing. For the rest of the dinner, the boys talked among themselves while Connie and Consuela ate and discussed their plans on how to make their lucrative business ventures more profitable. Their conversation was interrupted when they heard their front door get kicked open. In a split second, two masked gunmen entered. The two woman immediately sat up and told their boys to run to the hiding spot they had made in case anything like this ever was to happen.

"Y'all know what the fuck this is! Anybody move or talk, everybody die!" the gunman instructed. If his eyes weren't scary in itself, the chilling demeanor in the tone of his voice was sure to deliver fear into the hearts of his captives. With a gun in each hand, his partner reassured his comrade's statement, pointing his pistols directly at the Santana sisters' heads. Once compliance and order was established, gunman number one signaled his partner that he was going to search the house. Minutes later, he came back with Sha'Ron, Ka'Leaf, and Gus.

Ka'Leaf and Gus both had mean mugs on their faces, not showing any fear, but the youngest of the three, Sha'Ron looked terrified. He looked around in a state of confusion. At barely nine years old, he didn't have much of an understanding of the dangerous situation their entire family was in. His older brother and cousin, on the other hand, had already seen a few beat downs and standoffs when they'd gone with their mothers to "run errands." Sha'Ron started crying uncontrollably.

"Shut that motherfucking rug rat up before I do," one of the gunmen demanded impatiently.

"Fuck you," Ka'Leaf yelled at him as he stood up to the gunman. "Y'all bum-ass thieves better get the fuck outta our house."

"Yeah, y'all motherfuckers have no idea who the fuck you messing with coming up in our house." Gus backed his cousin up. Sha'Ron cried louder when he saw one of the men slap Ka'Leaf straight across his face. As soon as he went down, Gus went in with an uppercut, but the gunman was fast, and before he could even land his punch, the man swung his leg, and Gus flew in the air and landed hard on his back. With no regards nor sympathy, the other gunman then grabbed Sha'Ron and shoved him toward the twins.

Consuela grabbed her son, hugged, and kissed him. She promised him that everything was going to be OK. Hearing his mother's soothing voice seemed to calm Sha'Ron down a little bit. Consuela had seen enough. Never in her life has she been violated to this degree. Having been hustling for years, she understood that this was another part of the game, but to have the nerve to bring it to her front door and in front of their kids? That alone was an act that went against every rule and code that even the worst of the worst respected. There was no more keeping her composure. No more biting her tongue.

"Enough of this bullshit. Enough. Goddamn," she shouted at the gunmen while still holding Sha'Ron. "Violating me is one thing, but to terrorize my fucking kid? I promise to hunt you cowards down and—"

Boop! Boop! Two gunshots went off before she could finish the rest of her sentence. The first shot hit her in the chest. The other hit the child she held in his back. Both went crashing to the ground, still breathing, yet badly bleeding. Their injuries was serious enough to be fatal. Connie stared on in a state of disbelief. Seeing what these men had just done to her sister and nephew made her fear that she and the boys were next. She ran to the boys and pulled them in close and embraced them tightly. Prepared to die for her children, she shielded them with her own body as best as she could. If they did open fire, the shots would hit her first. The woman she was would die to protect her children. She loved her sister's sons as if they were her own. Before it got to that extreme, she decided to try to negotiate with the men.

"Wait a minute. Y'all don't have to do this. Please. You can have it all," she submitted cooperatively. Staring directly into the eyes of the man standing before her with his gun aimed directly at her and the boys, she noticed that her words had attracted his intention and interest. "If they don't get medical attention fast, they're going to die. The money can be made back; you can't get a life back. Please."

After a moment of odd silence, the gunman approached her and snatched her up by her neck. Ka'Leaf and Gus sprang into action and took that as their opportunity to try to run to the kitchen to grab a knife.

"Take one more step and I blow her motherfucking brains out," one of the gunmen yelled out. The boys stopped dead in their tracks and turned around to see Connie with a gun to her head. The other gunman walked toward the two cousins, pointed his gun at them, and guided them back to the dining room. It took every bit of strength Gus had not to fight, but his mother's life depended on it, so he followed instructions. The second gunman lifted his leg and kicked both of them to the floor.

"Y'all stay the fuck down there until I say you can get up," the first gunman said before returning his attention to Connie. "Now, why couldn't your sister shut her big fucking mouth and just give it the fuck up?" he wondered curiously. "You must be the smart one. So I tell you what, you have one chance, and only one chance, to save your family. If you do one stupid move, I will torture these two to death right in front of you while you watch. Now, lead the way."

Connie took him straight to the master bedroom of the house. Once there, she revealed to him where the hidden safe was located on the floor. To the naked eye, the hardwood floors appeared to be nothing out of the ordinary. However, at the entry of the walk-in closet underneath a Turkish rug, the wooden floor panels slid to the side, concealing a three foot wide hidden compartment. Discovering the compartment didn't necessarily mean one was able to remove the contents that it held. The high-tech safe only granted access when a matching handprint and security code was entered. The twins were the only people in the world that would be able to open that safe because their fingerprints were the only thing programmed in it. After Connie explained the process to the gunman, he first inspected it for himself. Upon her claims being confirmed, he pointed his gun at her head once again.

"I hope I made myself clear downstairs. You try anything stupid, the blood of your family will be on your hands," he warned her one final time before motioning her to open the safe.

There wasn't a doubt in her mind that the crazed gunman would carry out his threats if she didn't comply with his demands. Deep down inside, she honestly believed that even after she gave up everything in the safe that he was going to kill her and her family anyway. At that moment, she realized that the fate of her family lay with her. With her mind and heart racing faster than they ever had in her life, she slowly dropped down to her knees and placed her right hand on the screen of the safe. It took the safe's security system a few seconds to confirm and approve her identity.

"Please put in your access code," the robotlike voice requested aloud.

Taking a quick deep breath, she began to push in a sequence of buttons located on the keypad. The machine made a beeping sound with each number she entered. Other than that, there was an odd silence. That didn't last long at all. Suddenly, the entire house went completely dark. Along with the pitch-black darkness, a siren alarm sounded off throughout the home. It was nearly louder than a fire truck.

Fortunately for Connie, she'd remembered the code for the security feature that shut down all power in the house and sounded off the alarm. In that split second, she had to react. She removed a Glock 40 that was hidden next to the safe. She had to move quickly and quietly before the gunman moved. Otherwise, it'd be impossible for her to know the exact location of where he stood. The darkness made it nearly impossible for her to see anything at all. That is, until the gunman began shooting blindly around the room.

Big mistake.

Every time his weapon discharged, the fire spark from the chamber flashed enough light for her to see exactly where he was at. With her family's fate riding on her, she aimed and squeezed. Three shots was all it took. Each one hit their mark. Shots from her own gun provided light flashes as well. Certainly enough to see his forehead explode on impact by way of a .40-caliber slug. Before his body even hit the ground, she was on her feet running blindly down the back steps. By this time, her eyes were starting to adjust to the darkness. In addition, she also had the advantage of it being in her own home.

Having lived there for nearly three years, she knew the entire layout from room to room. She thanked God that she hadn't been shot when the man was firing aimlessly around the room. Halfway down the steps, she heard the screams and cries of Sha'Ron. Hearing his cries was like music to her ears. It was a sign that he was still alive. Even over the loud sirens, she could also make out Ka'Leaf's and Gus's voices.

"Auntie, please just hang in there," Gus was yelling.

"C'mon, Sha'Ron, you can't leave yet, baby boy," she heard Ka'Leaf's voice. With extreme caution she moved in the direction of the voices. It wasn't long before she spotted them. The boys were tending to Connie and Sha'Ron while the second gunman was looking around for an escape route. Connie wanted to put a bullet right in his dome, but it was too risky for her to come around the corner shooting while the boys were there. She couldn't risk them standing to their feet. Instead, she decided to run out of the side door of the house.

Once outside, she ran around to the front and hid on the side of the bushes. It was here that he was planning to make his escape. When he exited the house, she could hear him muttering under his breath that he should've shot all of them. Hearing this only further enraged her. She had to keep a level head and not let her emotions affect her actions right now. She took a deep breath and waited patiently until the perfect time for her to make her move. Once that moment arrived, she stepped out of her hiding place with phenomenal speed, like a snake striking without warning. Pressing her gun on the side of his temple, she fired her remaining shots. Even as he fell, she never took the gun from his temple, nor stopped firing. Standing over the top of his body, she stared at him for a moment before bending over and removing his mask. Although his head was badly deformed from trauma and bloodied, she still was able to recognize who it was. A taste so bad came to her mouth, she spat it out in the face of the man that fathered her only son. Ali! She hadn't seen or heard from him since Gus was a small baby, but yet, he came back in their lives, only to try to take them away and rob them of everything in the process.

It didn't take much thought for her to guess who the other dead gunman was. Atiff! He was Ali's twin brother. The foursome was once a loving twin couple, but greed and corruption got in the way of their relationships. The men became jealous when Connie and Consuela became better at their hustle then they ever were. They started accusing the girls of hiding money and trying to start their own hustle behind their backs. What they didn't realize was that the girls were ride or die, and they would've never crossed them like that. They just wanted more for their lives. Ali and Atiff were okay with just breaking into people's houses and making quick cash, but the girls were more business minded. They started flipping the money they made from the break-ins and buying bricks to sell on their own. They never hid anything from their men, but after months of arguing and accusations, one day, they both suddenly disappeared and weren't seen or heard from until now.

As Connie stood there trying to put the pieces of the puzzle together, it was as if time stood still, and she was moving in slow motion. Her thoughts were interrupted, and she snapped back into reality when she saw her son and oldest nephew emerge from inside the house. Gus carried her bloodied and injured nephew, while Ka'Leaf held a barely conscious Consuela. They were both seriously injured.

"Ka'Leaf, gently put her in the car. Gus, just keep holding him until we get to the hospital," she instructed the boys. They all carefully got into her car, and she drove them to the nearest hospital. Along the way, she begged God to keep them alive and fight for their lives. Even with the crisis in hand, she couldn't help but to notice about four or five responsive police cars racing toward the direction of their house. Deep down inside, she knew that once the cops got to the house and found the bodies, they'd ransack the place and discover the money and contraband. At this moment, she knew she and her sister would most likely get sent to prison for a long time.

"Gus and Ka'Leaf, I need y'all to listen and listen well. Whatever happens from here on, y'all stay together and always look out for each other. Remember, you can't trust nobody out here in these streets. There's always snakes in the grass, no matter how clean cut it looks. Always stay strapped and don't take no shit from nobody. We're all family. We bleed together, we fight together, we survive together."

"Ma, why you talking like it's all over? We gon' be all right." Gus tried to reassure her and himself in the same instance.

"Yeah, *Titi*, we gon' be okay," Ka'Leaf spoke up.

"You damn right we gon' be okay," she agreed with him. "We're Santantas."

Tears on top of tears fell from her eyes. Deep down inside, she knew it would just be a matter of minutes before the cops made their way to the hospital to cuff her and her sister regardless of her being shot or not.

She could've stayed back at the house and tried to clean everything out of the house, but that would have taken time. Time that could cost her sister and nephew their lives. For now, all she could do was breathe in her last few moments of freedom and spend them with her son and nephew.

In her heart, she knew she'd made the right choice . . . even if it cost her everything she had.

Mean Streets of Philly

Ten Years Later

A few mourners stood around the candles and teddy bears that marked the area where Li'l Reek was executed last night on Fifty-fourth Street. His mother was on her knees touching the area where his blood still stained the concrete. At that point, she let go of all hopes and denials that maintained the little bit of sanity that still existed within her. Without warning, she let out a loud horrifying scream—one that only the brokenhearted, stolen soul individuals can relate to. Several of his family members and friends rushed to her side with the intent to provide comfort, aid, and support. To no avail was their efforts. Nothing anyone said or did could bring her child back. The realization of that alone left her mentally, physically, emotionally, and spiritually ruined.

The site of the memorial had become one of deep sadness and grief as friends and loved ones bonded and grieved the senseless killing of their lost loved one. Among the many mixed feelings in the air, some wanted peace, others wanted justice, vengeance was promised, and, of course, everybody wanted answers. As if a dark gray cloud suddenly appeared and hovered over the memorial, the triple-white 750 BMW and its occupants had indeed possessed the same threats, dangers, and destructions as that of an unexpected, unpredictable storm. Pulling directly alongside the memorial, their thunderous sound system blasted over the crowd as if it was an outdoor concert. Gangster music echoed "Murder One" lyrics loud and clear for all to hear. The Clipse classical hood anthem, "What happened to that boy?" produced an obvious message to anyone that could read between the crafty violent punch lines. *"He was talking shit and we put a clap into that boy."*

Neither the luxury vehicle nor its occupants were a stranger to the mourners or the neighborhood. No introductions were necessary. These individuals needed no invite, permission, or inquiries. They made ways, broke rules, and did as they pleased, establishing order and control through murder, extortion, and intimidation. These men were none other than the infamous Santana boys. On the streets of Philadelphia they wreaked havoc, made money, and set examples of how to do it, how to take it, and how to keep it.

After a few minutes of observing the crowd from their vehicle, the doors on the BMW swung open. The three young men stepped out and walked through the crowd until they reached the exact spot where Li'l Reek was murdered. Each of them wore a white T-shirt with what appeared to be tributes to Li'l Reek's memory. Upon closer look, the true writings inscribed on the T-shirts brought about shock, fear, and disgrace. The front of the shirts read, "Rest in Peace." below a picture of Li'l Reek. Below the bottom of the picture the words "Kill All Rats." At that very moment, the smart ones among the mourners began to walk away. They didn't dare to protest, accuse, or defend. Ain't want to see nothing or hear nothing. But for the few that decided to stay and take "a stand" for their neighborhood and against violence, they would soon learn the consequences of their actions.

Ka'Leaf Santana, known in the streets as just Leaf, was the wildest of the family. His brother Sha'Ron and cousin Gus were shooters as well but not like him. Leaf was an animal. It was clearly displayed in his actions. After walking up to the pole where the mourners had placed teddy bears, candles, and balloons, he unbuckled his pants, pulled out his johnson, and urinated all over them. Li'l Reek's mother was the only one to defend her son's honor.

"You sick motherfucker. How dare you. How dare you. I know you killed my baby and—" Before she could speak another word, Leaf cut her off.

"Man, fuck this rat-ass nigga bitch," he said before removing his gun and shooting wildly over the heads and under the feet of the mourners that mistakenly stayed behind when they could have left. "Get the fuck off my block, crying over this bitch-ass nigga!" he screamed with agitation and hatred. The crowd dispersed and ran for cover. They were shocked, scared, and hurt that someone would bring more pain and grief to them during a terrible time like this. And just like that passing storm, after unleashing rain and fury, the Santanas disappeared into the darkness as fast as they appeared.

What Li'l Reek's family and friends didn't know was that there was a reason he was laid up in the morgue. A few nights ago, the police did a raid on a few blocks that the Santana boys controlled. Several workers were arrested and charged with drug possession. Li'l Reek was among those arrested. After being bailed out, two of the workers swore to Gus that in the middle of the night, a detective came downstairs at two in the morning and removed Li'l Reek from the cell. When he returned hours later, they said he smelled like cheesesteaks and Newports. In instances like this, it could only mean one thing.

Immediately after bailing them out, they were all ordered to come to the block for a meeting. Once there, everyone was given a chance to speak. When confronted with the accusations made against him, Li'l Reek broke down, crying and begging for mercy. His pleas fell on deaf and uncompassionate ears. To set an example to the rest of the workers, he was executed by Leaf in broad daylight. Shots to his head and face ensured that he would get a closed casket. Leaf felt as though Li'l Reek wasn't worthy of a proper traditional funeral.

Meanwhile, across town, Trish was just wrapping up a phone conversation with one of her girlfriends. Her friend was always up on the latest news, gossip, and rumors going around the neighborhood. The information Trish had just heard not only disappointed her but enraged her like never before. Having already texted Gus 911, she knew he'd be walking through that door any second. As she impatiently waited, she paced back and forth in the living room, anticipating the second he came walking through that door. When she saw his BMW finally pull up in the driveway, she rushed to the door to meet him. As soon as the door opened, the first thing she saw was the T-shirt. It only added more fuel to the fire.

"What the *fuck* is wrong with you, Gus? Are you using your fucking head? You niggas think y'all untouchable. If y'all don't get killed, y'all going the fuck to jail," she snapped. Her eyes started to tear up from that thought alone.

Trish and Gus had been together for four years and had been through a lot of ups and downs in that time. She was five feet eight, with a petite build, bronze complexion, hazel eyes, and long, curly hair. Although her frame was thin, she had hips that curved and a plump, round ass that could be seen from the front. Not only was she beautiful, but she had charm and brains to go along with it. She loved Gus, but she hated the way he behaved when he was with his cousins. It was as if they brought out an ignorant side of him. She knew he wasn't on the right side of the law when she got with him, but he didn't act like a typical street dude. He always treated her with respect and wasn't the type to walk around acting like a thug. Whenever he got with his cousins Sha'Ron and Leaf, though, he became a completely different person. She always feared the worst whenever he hung out with them.

Gus stood there at a loss for words. If it was one thing that he couldn't stand, it was to see his girl cry. Besides that, he hated how the streets talked and how fast word would get back to her. *Rats on top of fucking rats,* he mumbled softly. The smooth talker he considered him-self to be, he figured he could easily talk himself out of it. Producing his charming smile, he wrapped his arms around her waist and spoke softly.

"Come on, Trish, calm down, baby. It ain't even that deep," he calmly downplayed the situation.

"Not that deep? Gus, you're running around with your dumb-ass wild cousins shooting up everything, and then broadcasting it with these fucking T-shirts. What the fuck you mean it ain't that deep, Gus?"

"You're right, baby. I'm slipping. These fucking streets don't understand no other language. But I promise you this time, I'ma move different," he swore before remov-ing the T-shirt and throwing it in the trash.

"Gus, your mom left you in charge because you're a thinker. You've got to control them niggas. If you can't, cut them off. Because that's what your mom told me on the last visit, and I'm not trying to hear her fucking mouth. That shit make us look bad and incompetent."

He knew in his heart she was right. Women like her were hard to find, and he was very appreciative to have her in his corner. To express his love, he grabbed her by the waist and held on to her tightly while moving his hands through her hair. He found her lips with his and gently inserted his tongue into her mouth. The intense kissing quickly escalated. Once he removed the rest of his clothes, he did the same to Trish.

Starting at her neck, he placed soft, wet kisses all over. Making his way down, he caressed her breasts with his hands and gently took one of her nipples into his mouth. He then began licking at her nipples and used his fingers until they became hard. Trish couldn't take the anticipation. She wanted to feel the warmth of his mouth in her pulsating woman's cave. Pushing the top of his head downward, she didn't let go until his tongue was inside of her vagina. Even then, she grinded, stroked, and bounced until she came, holding the back of his head until he sucked every drop of it up. In exchange, she sucked on his manhood as if it was coated with sweet candies. The way she pleasured him, it didn't take too long for him to explode in the back of her throat. His favorite part was when she smacked his shaft against her tongue and slurped up any extras. Oral sex was just an appetizer. Rough sex always followed. Gripping her up roughly by the hair, just the way she liked it, he pushed her up against the wall. From this position, he was able to enter her on an upward angle. This stimulated her clit with each stroke, causing her eyes to roll to the back of her head with satisfaction. Their moans and wet sounds of sex were the only noises that could be heard through-out the house. As they shared a pleasurable orgasm, they stared into each other's eyes with ultimate satisfaction. To them, makeup sex was sometimes better than the traditional, everyday sex.

That night, Gus and Trish were relaxing in the living room watching a movie when out of nowhere, Trish shut the TV off and turned to face her man.

"So, are we going to finish what we were talking about earlier today?"

"What, babe? What are you talking about?" Gus acted like he had no idea what was going on, but when Trish looked at him like she was about to lose it, he became serious. "Trish, I know how you feel about Leaf and Sha'Ron. I'm gonna talk to them and tell them we need to be more low key," he reassured her.

"Gus, baby, I need you to be careful out there. You and your cousins act like y'all are untouchable, and that's dangerous. Look at what happened with your mom and aunt. They got lucky that the judge only gave them fifteen years. Your mom tells me all the time to keep you in check with all the shit you be doing out here. You think she doesn't know, but she has eyes everywhere." Trish had become very close with Connie over the past four years that she'd been with Gus. She had met Connie during one of Gus's monthly visits. Gus insisted that she come and meet his mother because he felt himself falling in love with her, and he refused to be with a woman that his mother didn't approve of. The two ladies hit it off from that first visit, and it wasn't long before Trish would write and visit Connie on her own.

"Trish, I gotchu. I don't know what else you want me to say. I know Mom and Titi Consuela expect me to look after Leaf and Sha'Ron. I been in charge and taking care of them since they got locked up. Why would I stop now?" Gus wasn't lying about his last statement.

Ever since his mom and aunt were arrested, he was forced to man up and take care of his little cousins. Sha'Ron was nine and Leaf was just a year younger than

Gus when the women were taken away, but Gus had always been the mature one of the two. He made sure to look out for his cousins when they were sent to foster, and when they tried to split them up a few years later, he ran off with them. His mother had left a large stack of money with a good friend of hers, and she was able to give Gus all of the information before they shipped her off upstate. With a good amount of cash, Gus was able to keep him and his cousins together and take care of them. As they grew older, though, that hustle mentality took over, and they decided to live up to their names and pick up where their mothers left off. They'd been ruling the streets for a few years now, and things couldn't be better.

"Gus, I love you, and I just don't want anything to happen to you out there," Trish said as she leaned in and gave him a soft kiss.

"I love you too, babe. Don't worry. I promise I'm gonna talk to the guys and get shit under control. I'm gonna start doing things different from here on out," he promised her.

Federal Detention Center: Philadelphia

"Connie, Consuela . . . Wake up, y'all! Fifty-fourth Street is all over the news. They said it's the seventh body this year up there, and now federal authorities are stepping in," said Monique after busting in their cell. Because she was one of the twins' closest associates they had in the jail, she was always welcome in their cell. Especially being it was a matter that concerned her family.

Connie and Consuela Santana were twin sisters raised on the streets of West Philadelphia. A mix of Cuban and Puerto Rican, their exotic features stood out and represented sheer beauty. Often referred to as "Queen Gangsters," the twins had had their fair share of good times and bad times. Ups and downs. Even though they were short "dime piece" classy women, they were down for the cause and always prepared to move. Barely standing four feet eleven, both had gorgeous, long, jet-black hair that hung slightly below their behinds. With the face of a goddess and curves like a Cola-Cola bottle, they were high commodities on the streets, as well as in prison. These were women that hustled and outhustled. Gunned and outgunned. Poor and rich. Standing tall for what they believed in earned them a fifteen-year sentence in the federal system. Charges stemming from murder to drug possession, firearm possession and money laundering. Connie was Gus's mother, and Consuela was the mother of Leaf and Sha'Ron. The sisters not only were twins, but were also best friends and cellmates finishing up their tenth and final year in Philadelphia's Federal Detention Center. They had been sentenced to fifteen years but were getting out in a few months due to good behavior and because they took some college courses while they were in there. It was all a part of an incentive program that they had for prisoners. If they showed that they were willing to behave and take courses to better their lives, it showed that they would be productive members of society. The twins had no intentions of having regular jobs when they were released, but they did whatever they had to do if it meant cutting their sentences down.

The twins watched in silence as the reporter spoke about the man killed in cold blood. The news was upsetting and disappointing. Not only were they just awakened from their sleep, but they knew their children were likely responsible for any shootings that took place on Fifty-fourth Street. Nothing went on without their knowledge. Just the mention of the feds gave them an adrenaline rush. They hated the feds. They had already learned the hard way just how vicious the feds were. Their current situation was proof of it in itself.

"Damn, Connie, didn't you tell Trish on a visit to let them crazy-ass fucking boys know to pipe down?" asked Consuela.

"Bitch, you know them hardheaded-ass niggas ain't trying to hear what nobody got to say," replied Connie as she brushed her teeth and washed her face.

"Well, we can't afford to have the feds' eyes on the boys. We damn near at the fucking door, yet they still out here killing shit. It's about time we made an OG call and reach out to someone that we can trust and show them what this life and hustling shit is really all about," said Consuela. Connie agreed.

Before stepping out of their cell, they discussed the matter at hand and came up with a well thought of solution. From the very beginning, their connect, Curtis "Black" Campbell, remained loyal and gave them his 100 percent support. He always reminded them that they were his heroes, and if ever they should need him for anything, to never hesitate to reach out. Today, they decided to cash in on that favor. In the feds, all personally placed phone calls were monitored and recorded. The only way around it was to place a legal call to your attorney. These calls were unmonitored. Client-attorney privilege. This was how the twins communicated their criminal activities. Upon placing their call, all it took was the mention of their last name. The receptionist acknowledged them immediately. After a brief conversation, she was connected to her attorney, Ken Edelin. Hands down, he was one of the best criminal attorneys around. "Courtroom Bully." was his well-earned nickname.

"Is this my girls? How you girls been in there?" he inquired.

"Hey, Ken. We've been good for the most part. We got a few months left before we go to a halfway house. But that's not the reason why I called," Connie explained.

"Well, what is it? Anything for you girls."

"Ken, I need you to reach out to Black and tell him I need him to take my son and nephews under his wing. They got a lot of learning to do, and I don't know a better teacher than him. Lastly, mention to him that he takes full responsibility for their successes, while I take full responsibility for any fuckups. Express to him that I'll be forever in debt to him for his intervention if he decides to accept my proposal," she explained.

"I'll have him stop by my office immediately. Don't worry a hair on your pretty little head. I'll make sure this matter is addressed ASAP. Is there anything else I can do for my favorite girls in the whole world?"

"No, that's it, Ken. Good looking. We'll make sure to be in touch," Consuela assured him before hanging up.

After placing the call, they both felt a sense of relief, confident that Black would consider their request and likely make good on his word. Here was a man of great character. Extremely powerful. Very influential. Best of all, he was highly connected, pushing keys since the eighties. Their only concern was how dangerous he was. And how wild and reckless their kids were. Could be a bad mix . . . Here was a man that managed to stay off the radar for years. He was once arrested by the feds for gun possession. However, the case was later dismissed for insufficient evidence. Behind closed doors, he ran and ruled the city with an iron fist. But in the eyes of the general public, he was a successful businessman.

For years he supplied the twins. They were his top customers, and they had a serious history together. Knowing how dirty the federal system worked, he was aware that the twins could have easily mentioned his name and made things easier on them. But they didn't. Although it was expected of them to stand tall, Black still praised them for it, and it was one of the main reasons he remained loyal. The twins felt comfort knowing Black would soon be looking after their boys. They questioned why they hadn't thought of asking him years ago.

Somewhere in West Philly

Driving through the hood in his black LS 450 Lexus, Black stared around the streets of his childhood neighborhood with disgust and disappointment. He felt proud of himself for getting out and becoming the successful man that he had become. Abandoned homes, crack addicts, fast-food restaurants, and liquor stores plagued the community. Most of the people he observed seemed hopeless, content, and poor. Sure, he could have contributed his hand in fixing it up and helping people in need out. However, most of them were customers of his workers, and in his mind, they weren't worthy of anything other than the drugs he prescribed. In his line of work, compassion and regrets were a weakness. Something he couldn't be or do. The ringing of his cell phone broke him out of the trance he was in and brought him back to reality. *Ken Edelin? What the fuck his greedy ass want?* he wondered before answering.

"Ken! The motherfucking 'devil's advocate.' I hope you ain't calling me with no bad news."

"No, nothing like that. Got a message for you. However, I'd rather discuss it with you personally if you're not too busy."

"All right. I'm in the area now. Give me about fifteen minutes," replied Black before disconnecting the call.

Black was the biggest thing coming out of Philadelphia. Previously and presently, he was a ruthless dictator. Boss, gangster, puppetmaster, and moneymaker were just a few words to describe the kind of man that he was. He walked and carried himself with pride. Standing at six foot four and weighing in at a solid 230 pounds of muscle, no one dared to ever go against him. His rich chocolate complexion, chiseled face, and almond-shaped eyes made many women chase after him. But one look into those almond eyes and you'd immediately see why he was feared by many. They say the eyes are the window to a person's soul, but Black was the exception. Looking into his eyes, you were met with a cold, sinister stare.

Having grown up in the streets all of his life, he had an arrogance about him, and people had no choice but to respect it. His parents, both crackheads, doped themselves to death when Black was just twelve years old. Black was lucky they hadn't killed him as a baby because they were addicts for as long as he could remember. He grew up living in an abandoned house with his parents. Then one morning when they never made it "home," he went looking for them and found them dead in an alley. He didn't bother to report it because he knew they'd put him into the system. He walked away without even looking back, leaving their bodies there for someone else to discover. He started from the bottom as a "lookout" boy, and he put in that work until he got to the top. As he made his way up, he learned the hard way not to trust people, even if they say they got your back. The only person he trusted was himself. If you weren't with Black, he automatically considered you an enemy.

He worked his ass off to get to where he was, and he didn't dare to ever let his guard down and have someone take it from him. Philadelphia was his city. Through blood, sweat, and tears, he most certainly had earned his spot. Murder, extortion, dealing, robbery—whatever it took—*nobody* was going to knock him off his pedestal. With each day he remained in power, he got more powerful. Each dollar built riches.

Thirty minutes after receiving the call from Ken, Black was walking through his office door. Ken briefed him about the phone call he received from the twins. Black sat back in the seat and registered everything he just heard. The twins were basically asking him to be a babysitter to some wild-ass juveniles. He'd heard and known about the Santana boys for a while now. Unbeknownst to them, he had been keeping track of them ever since their mothers had been picked up. The only reason he hadn't had his guys creep up on them already is because he had much respect for their mothers. Otherwise, he would've put a stop to their hustling and slinging a long time ago. Knowing what they went through as kids, he could understand why they were out here moving the way they did, and he respected that. The boys had heart, that was for sure.

As much as he didn't want to take three young hot-headed boys under his wing, he couldn't let Connie and Consuela down. The Santana twins were good people, and they had proven themselves to be loyal and tough as nails. They had the chance to snitch on Black all those years ago, and the fact that they didn't said a lot. If they needed a favor, he would have it handled. He had given them his word that if they ever needed anything, he'd have their backs, and a man like him would never go back on his word. His word was his bond, and he was prepared to die and kill for what he stood for. There was nothing he couldn't do.

Guiding some young niggas? This is gonna be easy, like pushing pawns up a chess board.

So he supposed.

1 . . . 2 . . . Feds Is Coming for You

Amy Tyler, a single mother of two children, had scored a high grade on her exam to become a federal officer. She had devoted herself to making a difference in her community, as well as the city. She had two weeks of training left before she would be in the field, and she couldn't wait. During her training, she had mastered psychology as well as several mind games that were considered strong tactics to break suspects and have them willing to tell on their mothers for a hope of a respectable release date. She had aced several exercises with flying colors. Her supervisors were very impressed and had already assigned her to lead an investigation into the drug-related murders in West Philly.

Over the past few years, the murder rate in Philadelphia had soared over 40 percent. There were now 415 bodies a year, making the city the murder capital of the United States. Handguns and assault weapons in the hands of criminals were common and overwhelming. The feds had no choice but to establish several operations to bring down the murder rate and get guns out of the hands of dangerous criminals. The feds began picking up any crimes where a gun was used. They would make sure that the suspects who were arrested for these crimes were facing outrageous time, and the only way to get a shorter sentence was to cooperate and get a 5K1 motion. This petition was filed by the United States District Attorney's office on behalf of their cooperating witnesses. Their plan to this day is genius and has helped the city solve thousands of murders, robberies, shootings, etc. It is said that over 80 percent of federal inmates are cooperating for shorter sentences, money, or to help an associate or loved one out of a jam.

Amy had high hopes of being able to make a difference in the number of arrests being made in Philly. The more arrests they made, the faster the murder rate could go down. She was excited to graduate in two weeks. She planned to hit the ground running. She'd dreamed about being a federal officer ever since her mother was shot and killed during a drive-by shooting. She would never forget the day her aunt came into her room and gave her the news that her mother had been killed. She felt sad, angry, confused, and determined, all in one. She was sad to have lost her mother, and she was angry that she was killed over a senseless street beef that had nothing to do with her. She remembers being confused and angry with God for having let this happen, but at the same moment, she felt determined to avenge her mother's death. She knew better than to try to go after her mother's killers. Her mother would never want her to become a street thug. Instead, she made a silent promise to become a person of the law and do her part to keep something like that from happening again. Putting away murderers was the best way for her to avenge her mother's death. Amy knew her mother would be proud.

As Amy studied the facts of her investigation, she learned that the alleged suspects were Gustavo Santana and Ka'Leaf Santana. This wasn't the first time she'd heard those names. The last name, Santana, had been known in Philly for years. She remembered reading about two twin sisters being arrested back when she was a teenager. She wondered if these boys were related to them. Amy decided the best thing for her to do is look into their history. The more she knew about their past, the better chances she had of knowing who their people were. It was important for her to know who they worked with, who they trusted, and how they operated. If she got lucky, she might even be able to get one of their workers to cooperate with her investigation. If she could catch the Santana boys, it'd be a great way for her to start her career in law enforcement.

Change Going to Come

"Turn the fucking music down, Leaf!" screamed Gus while giving Leaf a hard stare.

"What the fuck is up with you, cuz? You ain't never had a problem with me listening to this shit loud before. You been acting real funny since the other night, and I ain't feeling it. What the fuck is good?" growled Leaf returning the stare.

"My fucking problem is you always gotta do shit loud for everybody to hear. The streets is talking about the shit we did to Li'l Reek," Gus snapped, "Everybody and their mother know we murked him, and we really don't need all this unnecessary attention."

"I know you fucking around with me right now, cuz. You ain't say shit when we were on our way to the spot, and we showed up wearing those shirts and blasting that song," Leaf clapped back. "I bet your bitch-ass girl got in your head with all this shit."

"Watch how you talk about my girl." Gus stepped into Leaf's face.

"Oh, it's like that, Gus? You gonna fight your own blood over some pussy?" Leaf said in between clenched teeth. "Let's go then, cuz," he said, ready to fight. He knew deep down Gus wasn't going to fight him, though. They grew up like brothers, and they'd promised each other years ago they'd never fight each other, especially over a female. "Bros before hoes" was their motto.

"Man, you know we ain't gonna square off," Gus said as he sucked his teeth and backed up. "I'ma tell you once, though, don't talk about Trish like that. She ain't like other bitches I've fucked with."

"All right, I can respect that," Leaf said as he put his hands up. "But what's really good, cuz? Why you walking around like you got a chip on your shoulder?"

"It ain't got no chip. I just been thinking about things lately, and we really need to change shit and step up our game. We can't be out here flossing and showing off, or else we gonna get attention from the boys in blue, and you know that's the last thing we need. I wasn't left in charge to do stupid shit and be sloppy. You know our moms is getting out soon, and we need to have our shit ready for them. We're Santanas, goddamn it," Gus said, giving Leaf a speech that was inspired by Trish.

Leaf had no choice but to listen to everything Gus was saying because he could tell his cousin was in his feelings right now, but he didn't agree with everything he was talking about. Leaf wasn't a lay-low type of guy. Leaf was the type of nigga that got excited by murders, shootings, and going to war with rival crews. He thought the complete opposite of what Gus was saying. He felt it was important to let people know and see the shit they were capable of doing. He wanted to show everyone that the Santanas were not to be played with or taken lightly.

"Nah, man. Motherfuckers out here need to know who the fuck we are. The fuck I look like, keeping shit in secret like I'm scared? I ain't scared of nothing," Leaf said, raising his voice.

Gus knew this wasn't going to be an easy conversation with his cousin. Leaf was a hotheaded-act-on-sight type of guy. He was a man of few words and all about action. That's why he was considered the enforcer, and Gus was the thinker.

"Leaf, you need to—"

"Yo, what are y'all arguing about now?" Sha'Ron walked into the living room, interrupting Gus midsentence.

"This nigga over here telling me we need to lie low like we some scared bitch-ass cowards." Leaf let his brother in on the conversation.

"Oh my God, Leaf. I swear, you always gotta blow everything out of proportion. I never said we need to hide from nothing or nobody," Gus snapped again. "All I'm saying is we gotta be careful that we don't get too much attention and have the alphabet boys come after us."

Sha'Ron just stood there and looked back and forth between the two men. Being the "baby" of the family, Sha'Ron was a good blend of both his cousin and his brother. He knew how to handle himself with weapons, but he'd learned to keep his cool and not be so quick to react. Over the years, he'd become somewhat of a peace-keeper in the house, often having to step in between Gus and Leaf to keep them from arguing so much.

"All right, all right, both of y'all need to calm down," he spoke up. "Leaf, all Gus is saying is when you pop off, make sure ain't too many people watching, because you know there're rats everywhere, and they always looking to get some cheese, so they'll be quick to snitch us out."

"Exactly," Gus agreed with his little cousin.

"Gus, it's a little too late for us to try to lie low. You must be forgetting about all the motherfuckers laid up in boxes and suits because of us. You don't think their people know it was us, and are trying to get even? Man, if a motherfucker try to get the drop on me . . . I'ma body them and everything they love," promised Leaf while lifting his shirt to expose the P90 with extended clip. "I don't give a shit who's there to see it."

"Listen, nigga, bottom line, no more fucking bodies . . .
right now. If a nigga come at you, do what you should,
but only if a nigga try to line you up. Moms called me
a week ago, went off on me about what they saw in the
news about us rolling up at Li'l Reek's vigil and shit. Now,
both my mom and your mom must think we out here
incompetent of running the family business because the
day after I talked to her, I got a call from their lawyer
telling me that their friend, that old head nigga Black, is
looking for me, talking about wanting to have a sit-down.
I got to show them that I'm still, and always have been,
capable," explained Gus.

"Yo, for real?" Sha'Ron questioned.

"Yup, now I'm gonna have to take time out and sit
with that nigga and probably have to listen to him try to
school me like we ain't been out here doing shit on our
own for years."

"Well, damn, cuz, you shoulda said all that shit from
the beginning," Leaf said, now understanding where Gus
was coming from. "A'ight, I gotchu," he said, extending
his hand to give his cousin a pound. The two connected
fists and almost immediately, you could feel the tension
leave the room.

"Can I go back to playing my music? Shit, you really
good at fucking up a nigga's vibe," Leaf said as he play-
fully shoved Gus and turned back to press Play on the
iPod.

"Yea, Negro, you can play your music now," Gus replied.
Gus wasn't entirely convinced that Leaf was on board
with what was said, but he decided to leave it alone for
the time being.

"Well, while you old heads stay home listening to your
music and whatever else old people do, I'm gonna go
get my dick sucked and beat some pussy up," Sha'Ron
exclaimed. "Look at that fine-ass bitch I got waiting

in the car." He walked Gus and Leaf toward the living room window so they could see this cute, light-skinned, Spanish-looking girl sitting in his white CL55 Mercedes.

"A'ight, young buck. Do your thing, bro," Leaf said, giving his brother dap.

"Stay strapped and wrapped," Gus put his two cents in.

The Meet-Up

The house Gus had been directed to was breathtaking. It reminded him of a small castle. It had a modern Victorian kind of vibe to it. As he pulled into the driveway, he couldn't help but to notice the small fleet of foreign vehicles lined up back-to-back. Benz, Beemer, Lexus, Range. *From the looks of it, this nigga got that sack for sure. Picture me with a plug like him. We'll see.* As he approached the front door of the house, the door swung open. Standing in the doorway was an attractive light-skinned woman wearing a pastel blue bikini thong swimsuit. Waving him inside, she stepped aside so that he could enter. There wasn't much space for him to go around. Their bodies brushed up against each as he squeezed himself through. With a flirtatious smile, she looked up and down before motioning for him to follow her. As she led the way through the house, he took a quick look around. A few females sat around a movie projector watching movies and smoking exotic. They all wore bikinis as well.

When they reached the back of the house, Gus was led through double-wide French doors that gave way to a perfectly manicured backyard patio. From there, he could see Black seated at the captain's chair inside what looked like a ten-man Jacuzzi. He was in the middle of a telephone conversation. Gus noticed that the cell phone he talked on was anything but basic. It was five times bigger and had a thick black antenna. It was indeed high tech. He took a moment to study his surroundings. There was a nice-size swimming pool, a basketball court, as well as a tennis court. For a first impression, Gus was very impressed. The woman that had walked him out went inside and quickly returned. She handed him a towel and a pair of swimming trunks.

Gus seemed a little confused at first. He thought he was coming for a regular sit-down. He wasn't expecting for the sit-down to be in a Jacuzzi. What he didn't know was that Black was a very calculated man. He usually held first meetings in the pool or the Jacuzzi; it forced people to have to strip down, and it would expose anyone that came wired. Gus took the swimming trunks and changed in the pool house. When he came out, Black was now accompanied by two gorgeous women. From what Gus could see, they were completely nude. One of the women had the most perfect breasts he'd ever seen. They had a teardrop shape, and her nipples looked like Hershey kisses.

"So we finally meet," Black said as he gestured for Gus to have a seat. As soon as Gus entered the hot Jacuzzi and sat down, the powerful jet streams immediately began to relieve the tension in his back and shoulders.

"How you doing, Old Head? I'm Gustavo Santana. I'm sure my mother has spoken to you about me."

"Yes, she has," Black responded. Just as Gus was about to speak, one of the Cambodian girls whose name was Sophia came close to Gus and attempted to put her hand on his manhood. He quickly reacted by grabbing her hand and placing it to her side before addressing Black.

"Old Head, you think I can holla at you personally for a few moments?" Black gave the girls a head nod, and they both got out of the Jacuzzi. As tempting as it was to have the woman stroke him to ecstasy, he wasn't here for that. Watching the two beauties walk out of the Jacuzzi, exposing their completely shaved pink pussies and plump, round asses, Black let out a loud whistle.

"I ain't never seen a nigga turn down Sophia. What's your secret?" asked Black, seeing if Gus would pass his first test.

"I got a girl, Old Head. Sis pretty and all that, but she ain't on my chick level. Plus, I don't mix business with pleasure," Gus replied, passing Black's test with flying colors. Black was glad to see Gus wasn't the type to get distracted by ass and titties. Plus, Black had already done his homework on Gus. He knew all about his girl Trish, and to refuse Sophia showed discipline, restraint, and loyalty . . . characteristics of a real nigga. They talked about everything from the twins, to the streets, to the game, and to the ultimate goal. He took an immediate liking to Gus. He admired his style and could see he possessed the heart and intelligence it took to be a true leader. The fact that he could go deep into conversations about business aspects, developments, and investments left Black mighty impressed.

A few minutes before wrapping their conversation up, Sophia came back out of the house carrying a huge lit blunt smelling of exotic weed. The other Cambodian girl carried a tray with a bottle of Moët and some champagne glasses. When Sophia passed the blunt to Gus, he declined.

"I don't smoke, ma. And I don't drink when I'm handling business." Surprisingly, he aced all of Black's tests. Black was very impressed with this young buck. He couldn't help but to smile from ear to ear. Gus reminded him of a younger version of himself.

Later that night, while Gus was driving back home, his eyes were on the road, but his mind was focused on another road, "The Road to Success." After seeing how the old head Black was living, he had a new inspired motivation. He felt determined to work hard and achieve that same kind of success. He just had to get his cousins on board and keep Leaf in check so he won't fuck shit up. Feeling excited for his future, he speed-dialed Trish on his cell phone.

"Hello," answered Trish on the third ring.

"What's good, girl? Get dressed. We are going out to the Cheesecake Factory."

"Oh yeah? I guess things went okay at your little meeting because I can hear it all in your voice."

"Just have your sexy ass dressed and ready when I pull up," said Gus.

That night, they enjoyed a delicious shrimp and chicken jambalaya dinner and ordered a few rounds of their favorite drink there, the Mai Tai. Gus filled her in on everything that had happened at Black's place. He conveniently left out the part about the naked women in the Jacuzzi. They were always honest with each other, but he knew better than to tell her he was surrounded by naked, beautiful women. He expressed to her how inspired he was to take his business to whole new level. She was excited for him, but deep down, she wished he'd stop the street hustle and start a legal business for himself. She wasn't ready to have that kind of conversation with him yet, though, so for the time being, she listened to him speak and promised him to always stay by his side, no matter what.

Later on back at home, Trish took full advantage of Gus's generosity and good mood. Once she got out of the shower, she splashed her body with cucumber and melon body fragrance. She wore nothing but a towel back to the bedroom. The day's excitement must have tired Gus out because he was knocked out sleeping. That didn't stop her one bit, however. She reached over toward the strawberry cheesecake slice they had brought back from the restaurant. She smeared some of it on her nipples and climbed on top of him so she could put her breasts in his face. She kept gently brushing her nipples along the lining of his lips, enticing him to wake up and join in.

He woke up and took one nipple into his mouth. He made his tongue bend, curl, and flick, allowing it to tease his woman, causing her to beg him to make his way toward her pussy. He grabbed more of the cheesecake and placed some right over her clitoris. He stroked his tongue up and down while Trish squirmed and moaned. He explored every nook and cranny of her insides. As her body started to shake violently, he stuck his middle finger inside her, causing her to explode her climax all over his face. She climbed off of him and lay on her side of the bed where she continued to moan and come from the aftershock. Gus lay on his side of the bed with a smile on his face. After all this time, he still knew how to satisfy his woman. He could have gotten up and fucked her mercilessly, but instead, he let her enjoy the moment. His pleasure was hers.

Over the next few weeks, Black kept close observation on the young Santanas. He didn't care too much for Sha'Ron and Leaf, but with proper guidance, Gus had potential to make some real money. The next time they got together, he planned to welcome him in with open arms and also give him strong advice on how to deal with his wild, careless cousins. He would make it clear that they were not his responsibility or concern. He was only taking Gus under his wing. So, however Gus chose to deal with them was up to him. There were a few ground rules he would give Gus that were never to be compromised or broken; the penalty was always paid with a life.

And So It Begins

Gus and Trish left their home dressed like they were members of a Fortune 500 company. Gus wore a navy-blue Kenneth Cole slim fit suit with an all-white button-up shirt and a metallic black skinny tie. Trish wore a black Oleg Cassini lace mermaid dress to complement her man's outfit. Tonight, Gus was to have his second meeting with Black. Black had invited him and his girl to his second home a few hours outside of Philly. Gus was anxious and a little nervous to be meeting with Black again. He had no idea what it was that Black wanted to discuss in this second meeting, but he was prepared to ask Black to let him work alongside him and his empire.

Tonight was the night Gus would hopefully take the first step into Bosshood. He had been anticipating this ever since the day he met Black. When Black called and told him and Trish to dress fancy and pack a few days' worth of outfits, Gus could only assume this was going to be a positive meeting. If everything went well during this meeting, he was about to be connected with one of the biggest plugs in the city. Gus had done his homework and looked into who Black was. He learned about what he came from and how he built his successful and lucrative empire. He also got a lot of insight about Black from his mother and aunt.

Hoping to make an everlasting impression himself, Gus and Trish packed their suitcases with the flyest linens they could afford. True Religion jeans, Prada belts, and Christian Louboutin shoes were all packed up and ready to go. They both wore their matching his and her Rolex watches. Trish wore her diamond chandelier earrings and her Gregg Ruth canary-yellow and white diamond pendant necklace. Gus wore his white gold diamond link chain.

Gus and Trish sat patiently waiting to get the phone call that would instruct them where they were to go. Gus's phone finally rang, and he was given instructions and directions to the location where the meeting was to take place. The person on the phone explained to Gus that he was to tell no one of tonight's meeting, nor was he to tell anyone of his whereabouts. Gus gave his word that this would be kept between him and his girl. Doing this, he knew that his word and name were on the line.

After passing the King of Prussia Mall and turning down a road, the streets got really dark. The only light was provided by the large homes that seemed newly built in the area. It was a little difficult finding the location because he wasn't given any street names, just instructions . . . *when you get there, make a left, go two blocks up, turn right, go straight and park.* Eventually, he came upon a huge single house. Gus knew better than to call back and ask for directions again. He had to show Black that he was capable of following directions and doing shit right the first time. Gus was anxious and excited to learn what this was about.

The house he had been directed to was fly as a motherfucker. He and Trish were in awe of the large house before them. The house had a warm and inviting feel with a lighted driveway. As the couple walked toward the front double doors, they passed a security sign, with another attached that read, 24-HOUR SURVEILLANCE MONITORING. Before he could ring the bell, the doors opened up, and a man greeted them. He stared Gus up and down for a few odd seconds, then looked over at Trish, smiled, and opened the door invitingly. He told the couple to follow him. Gus and Trish were led through a two-story foyer with a marble floor. Trish looked up and was mesmerized by the Swarovski crystal chandelier that hung from the vaulted ceilings. Gus was trying very hard not to stop and look around the house. He didn't want to get caught gazing.

As they made their way farther inside the house, they were even more taken aback by everything they saw. Black's home was fabulous. A black leather sofa covered the entire living room from wall to wall. A movie projector hung from the ceiling, feeding a clear picture to the 75-inch screen hanging above the fireplace. The floors in the living room were bamboo, and so was the frame of the miniature bar that housed top-shelf liquor, wine, and champagne. A beautiful, tall, Amazon goddess-looking woman entered the room and walked toward the couple. The woman reminded Trish of Kimora Lee Simmons.

"Hello, everyone. I'm Chyna, Black's wife," she said as she extended her hand toward Gus. "You must be Gus," she said. Gus took her hand and gently kissed it like a true gentleman would. She then turned over toward Trish and leaned in to give her a warm embrace. "And you must be Trish."

She offered them a drink and assured them that Black would be joining them soon so they could head out. Moments later, Black made his grand entrance into the living room sporting a black suit similar to Gus's, complemented by a dark brown fine mink with matching ostrich shoes. He extended his hand to Gus and afterward, he placed Trish's right hand into his and planted a soft kiss.

"You have a good man here. The day I met him, he spoke about you with hope, honor, and respect . . . It's a pleasure to meet you," said Black, giving Trish the feeling that she was married to the mob for real.

After engaging in a little small talk, they exited the condo. Outside was a black Mercedes-Benz Maybach with a private driver awaiting the two couples. This was normal for Black and Chyna, but Gus and Trish had never experienced luxury on this level. Laid up in that Maybach was sickening; it had the TVs that showed the perimeter of anything and everything within ten feet of the car. There were curtains in the windows and a stocked minibar. *This is the life,* thought Gus.

When they arrived at a private airport, Gus and Trish grabbed each other's hands. They couldn't help but to feel butterflies in their stomachs.

"Did you bring your passports like you were instructed?"

"Yes, we did," Gus replied. "Now are you going to tell us where we're going?"

"Not quite yet. We're going to one of my favorite spots. Trust me, you'll love it," Black said as a grin spread across his face.

After being led through the airport and down a private terminal, they were seated in a fully loaded G5 that Black claimed was owned by one of his family members who played professional sports in the city. Trish and Gus were left speechless by the jet's interior. White leather massage seats. Stocked bar. Marble floors and panels. Flat screen TVs assembled along the front row from every which position.

"We're going to be in the air for a few hours. Please, make yourselves comfortable and don't hesitate to ask if you get hungry or want anything to drink," Chyna said as she took her seat.

Later on in the flight, while Gus and Trish were sleeping, Trish was awakened by what she believed was some kind of physical confrontation, only to wake up and see

Black's naked body long stroking Chyna as she bent over the seat, holding onto whatever she could grip. Trish pretended to be asleep as she peeked at Black's huge dick popping bubbles and gushing juices in and around Chyna's pussy. Her pussy got soaked from just watching the erotic scene. The passion and pleasure Black and Chyna shared was so powerful that it made Trish come all in her panties, right along with them.

After hours of flying, the pilot gave warning to the passengers that they should buckle their seat belts and prepare for landing. After landing safely at Brazil's International, they were driven to a beach house owned by Black. It was all white and resembled a villa. It was so close to the ocean, you would throw a rock into it from right off the porch. Gus and Trish were mesmerized by the level of luxury Black acquired and lived. He made these types of impressions just to get those types of reactions.

"Y'all enjoying this shit yet, little homie?" he asked while motioning his hands around the island and his beach house. "I figured you could use a quick getaway to clear your head. Plus, I wanted to holla at you about something important anyway."

"For sure, ol' head. I definitely needed to be reminded of what I need to do and where I needed to be. This here was a up-front view of what I needed to see. I'm ready to turn shit up. All I really need is the right people behind me," Gus said. The way he put it, Black was sure to read between the lines.

"That sounds about right. Patience, brains, and dedication is what it really takes. We'll get into that later on," he insisted, before changing the conversation. "Leave all your worries behind. Let's go inside and make our way to the back dining room patio. Chyna made dinner arrangements before we even left the States and instructed our house cook, Dolores, to prepare a seafood feast for us."

Black and Gus made their way toward the back of the house to find Chyna and Trish already sitting at the table. Black wasn't kidding when he said there would be a seafood feast. On the table was an assortment of crab legs, scallops, jumbo shrimp, and lobster tails. Gus looked to his left and saw a middle-aged woman walking toward the table carrying a tray of Porterhouse steaks.

"I prepared these for if you want too." She had a thick accent, and she did her best to communicate in English.

"*Obrigada,* Dolores." Chyna thanked her in Portuguese. "Everything looks amazing." She complimented the cook. The two couples enjoyed their seafood and steak dinner. They made small talk while they ate. The sides were just as delicious as the steak and seafood. They had a selection of veggie delight: roasted mushrooms, corn, peppers, onions, wild rice, string beans, garlic mashed potatoes, and truffle macaroni and cheese. The foursome drank a few bottles of Moët and shared a delicious upside-down pineapple cake. After their meals were completed, Mrs. Dolores came out of the kitchen to ask if there was anything else she could do for them before she dismissed herself for the night.

Chyna, again, complimented her on her delicious cooking and handed her a huge wad of bills before telling her she could have the rest of the night off. The four of them left the table stuffed and satisfied.

The night was capped off with a few more drinks, a toast, and a walk alongside the ocean. Black was still speaking hopeful of the future, and that was all that mattered to Gus. When they returned to the house, Black announced that he would be retiring for the night. He informed them that he had an important day ahead of him. Everyone returned to their rooms. Certainly, it wasn't for sleep. There was something about the island and the ocean that made one's hormones rage. If anybody was to walk in a twenty-foot radius of the house, they was sure to be in for an earful.

The following morning, breakfast was brought to the bedrooms. It was an assortment of Brazilian pastries, fresh squeezed orange juice, steaming hot coffee, and spinach and feta cheese omelets. The maid that delivered the breakfast trays also handed Gus an envelope addressed to him and Trish with a private message from Black.

"Damn, Gus, how do you feel about all of this?" Trish asked him after reading the note. "I think the nigga going to surely put you on. Either way, I'm always down for you," she promised sincerely.

"You know I know that. You're Bonnie, baby, and I'ma always be your Clyde. I feel like good shit is in the works for me. But either way, one way or another, I'm going get to the top," he swore.

An hour later, the four of them were seating themselves in the white Range Rover that Black's driver had picked them up in. Black instructed his driver to stop at Ferno's. It was a popular nightclub on the island that Black had his hands in. When they pulled up in the parking lot, there were only four or five cars parked there.

"I'll be back in ten minutes," Black informed them before removing a small black bag from under the seat.

No more than five minutes later, Gus heard what sounded like powerful engines gunning up the road toward the parking lot. As the sounds got closer, about five trucks pulled into the parking lot. The screeching tires spread dust everywhere since the parking lot was unpaved.

"What the fuck!" Gus reached for the door to try to make a getaway as soon as he saw red and blue lights flashing through the headlights of the Suburbans and Yukons. "Trish, we need to get the fuck up outta here!" he yelled out as he reached for her with his other hand. Before they could even jump out, several masked men ran up on the Range Rover while the other men hopped out and ran inside the club.

"Nobody move. Get out of the car and face down on the ground!" one of the men instructed everyone. The men identified themselves as FBI and began frisking Gus and the driver. Trish was frozen in place, terrified of what was going on. She lay on the ground praying that everything would turn out okay. She had a million questions, but she knew better than to say a single word. She'd seen enough on the news of people getting killed by police for much less, and she was not trying to have her name added to that list. She refused to become another hashtag. Within seconds, a voice came over the fed's walkie-talkie.

"We got the fucking mother lode," was heard through one of the walkie-talkies. "We finally nailed the bastard. Take everyone in. The first one to talk gets the deal." Within what felt like seconds, they were all blindfolded, cuffed, and thrown in the back of a truck.

Twenty minutes later, Gus sat in a cold room, still blindfolded and cuffed to a chair. He was shocked and confused. He didn't know what the fuck he had gotten himself caught up in, and the silence in the room was killing him. He was questioning if maybe Black had set him up. The last two days had felt like a dream, and he was beginning to wonder if it really had all been too good to be true. As he sat there trying to piece shit together, he heard a door suddenly open.

"Well well well, Gustavo Santana." Gus was finally able to see when the blindfold was snatched off of him. His eyes immediately adjusted, and he saw two men standing directly across from him. A steel table was all that was between him and the two men.

"I guess you were trying to take over the family business, huh?" one of the men asked.

"You paid Black a substantial amount of money to purchase one hundred kilos, and he's willing to testify to it . . ."

"Well, if you got all that, send me to the jail so I can get dug in. Y'all got all the answers so why the fuck are you questioning me?" Gus replied with an attitude. The agents both let out a wicked laugh.

"You have us confused. Black already told us your aunt and mother contacted him from jail and told him to plug you in with his connects. It's already been confirmed. Now, we have reason to believe you have information about some shootings and murders you and your cousins were involved in back in the States. If your information leads to an arrest and conviction, we'll help you out with a great deal, but you have to help us help you," stated the fed.

"Maybe you dickheads ain't understand me, I don't *speak rat*. And one thing is for sure about the Santanas, we've always been financially secure and represented by the best, so your allegations will be addressed in court, so *fuck you and fuck your help*."

With that being said, the agents punched, smacked, and kicked Gus for five minutes straight before exiting the room. An hour later, they came back in with a small stack of papers in their hands.

"Trish . . . That's a very special woman you have there. She can't believe you chose jail over her. Don't worry; I'll take care of that little sweet black ass while Bubba is taking care of yours. You should have seen how fast she signed these statements about coming here to purchase one hundred keys and about your family in exchange for her freedom," said the fed while pushing Trish's statements over so Gus could see for himself. The other fed pushed Black and Chyna's statement over as well.

Gus read over the papers and although he was heart-broken, he didn't let it show. Instead, he built up as much spit as he could in his mouth and spit on the face of the fed who beat him the hardest. Gus started to brace himself for another beat down as the agents charged at him. Suddenly, the door flew open and Gus heard a familiar voice.

"Jack, Jill . . . *That's enough!* Thank you," said Black while entering the room. Gus sat there confused for a moment until he put it all together.

"That was some bullshit, Black, and I ain't like it, but I respect it."

"In this business, you can never be too certain or sure of someone until they're put into an uncomfortable situation. You passed all my tests, especially this one. Many people die in this very room because they were willing to compromise who they claimed to be just to get out of a jam at someone else's expense. But you stood strong and stood for who you are. As a token of my appreciation, it would be an honor to officially welcome you into my family. Now, come on out of here . . . Everyone's waiting on you," announced Black, leading Gus to where everyone was gathered.

"Hold on, Black," said Gus stopping in his tracks.

"First of all, it's an honor to be among your family, but it had nothing to do with how I carried myself in that situation. That there was expected of me, and I'll forever live by it and die by it. Now, please, take me to see my girl. She got me all the way fucked up. I really thought she'd snitched me out." Black and Gus chuckled at what had just happened. Gus wiped a little bit of blood that trickled from his lip, and his body was hurting, but his pride was helping him overlook the pain he felt. He was officially a part of the Black Squad, and he was sure the sky was the limit for him now.

***

Months after that final test, Gus was on top of his game more than he'd ever been in his life. Not only had he made the transformation from an average hustler to a business-minded entrepreneur. He also reconstructed his team in the process. Leaf was no longer indulging in street wars or unnecessary killings; he was now the family's chief of security. He touched no drugs and only moved out if it was necessary and approved. Sha'Ron was in charge of maintaining the product and distribution. He had refined his duties to a science, and the product was always consistent, which gave their street credibility a high rate of satisfaction. Gus was head of the family, as well as head of finances. He made sure his team was paid equally, and the money was laundered and profited through investments.

Black had grown very fond of Gus ever since bringing him to the table. He'd proved to be an asset and a hell of a student. One thing Black loved about him was that he was a good listener and Gus used his advice as a tool to conquer the streets. Although Black only had a daughter, he was beginning to love Gus as if he were his own son. And, whenever he would introduce Gus to one of his associates, he would say, "This is my favorite young buck." Black was close to retiring from the drug trade, but at the rate Gus was going, he figured one or two more years would make him at least a couple of million dollars richer.

Streets Is Watching

A clear shot of Gus's face appeared through the scope. Next, the image was locked in, followed by at least twenty shots. Amy sat in the backseat of the Explorer, relieved that she finally captured live shots of her target as he got out of his 750 BMW, talking on his cell phone and unaware that his every move was being monitored in one way or another. His house phone and cell phone were tapped, and he was being followed almost twenty-four hours a day. However, so far, Amy had nothing linking him to anything criminal. It was common sense that he couldn't afford to drive a BMW and own a house with no job, but proving where the money came from was going to be harder than she had originally anticipated.

So far, she had seen or heard nothing that tied him in with any criminal activity. *I wonder if they got tipped off by an agent. I need to get inside. Who do they trust? Who can get me inside?* Amy had been driving herself crazy trying to figure out how she was going to crack this case. A few months had passed since she'd graduated and officially been on the case, and she still had nothing to show for it. She was becoming obsessed with the case, ignoring everything else that fell on her desk. During her training at the academy, she was warned to be careful and not bring work home, but Amy found it impossible to leave this case at the office. It was all she thought about.

Every day, she would pick up her kids from day care and head straight home so she could keep studying every fact she had on her case. One way or another, she was determined to close her case. Gustavo Santana had a mark on his head, and she couldn't wait to pull the trigger.

The Homecoming

January 10, 2005, the Federal Building of Philadelphia's parking lot looked like a Cash Money music video was being filmed. However, that wasn't the case. Instead, major niggas throughout the city flooded the parking lot in fancy cars and mink coats awaiting the release of Connie and Consuela Santana. Their sons stood in front of two Range Rovers, one white and the other black, both brand-spanking-new off of the lot. Their release was ten years in the making.

At 12:00 p.m., the front doors to the prison visiting room opened up and the twins strolled out. Connie was dressed in a cream Chanel dress with matching glasses and shoes, while Consuela was dressed in a red and black Gucci dress with matching shoes and glasses. When their sons saw them, they ran up and helped them into their chinchilla coats. They then exchanged long, warm hugs. The twins were so overwhelmed with joy that they cried as their sons escorted them over to the cars.

As soon as the twins made their way to the parking lot, everyone cheered and clapped in celebration of their release. Shortly after, numerous people came up to pay their respects with hugs and envelopes full of money. The inmates in the jail went crazy, banging on their windows as they viewed the scene from the inside. The twins were overwhelmed and appreciative of how everyone had shown up to show their love and respects.

As much as they wanted to go straight to their sons' house, unfortunately, the twins had to report directly to the halfway house. That was to be their home for two weeks. The twins were disappointed when they'd been told they weren't completely free yet, but they figured they'd waited ten years for this moment. They could suck shit up for two more weeks. Their sons supplied them their bank cards and cell phones before they departed. They waved their good-byes to all the supporters before hopping into their Rovers and pulling off.

Shoot for the Moon
If You Want to Find Stars

"Jihad Cooper, report to the staff office . . . Jihad Cooper, report to the staff office," stated the correctional officer over the loudspeaker at Graterford State Prison. Jihad was in the middle of a dice game when he heard his name being called. *What a perfect time*, he thought. *Shit, I'm up 200 packs and that's a perfect opportunity to leave with my winnings before the tables turn against me.*

When he finally made it to the officer's station, they notified him that he had a visitor. He wasn't expecting any lawyers, and he knew it wasn't concerning any of his appeal motions because he hadn't filed any yet. Serving a forty-to-fifty-year sentence for attempted murder and third-degree murder. Having only served five years of his bid so far, his expectations of getting any good news was the furthest thing from his mind. Jihad wondered if maybe his homeboy Leaf was paying him a surprise visit. It'd been a few months since Jihad had heard from him. Jihad and Ka'Leaf had been close friends since they were young bucks. The shooting skill Ka'Leaf had was mostly because of Jihad. Jihad was the same age as Gus, but they never clicked as hard as he and Leaf did. Jihad's father had been OG marksmen back in the day, and he taught Jihad everything he knew. He would take Jihad out to the gun range every week and give him one-on-one lessons. Jihad would then turn around and show Leaf everything he learned. Leaf knew he wouldn't be the sharpshooter he was if it hadn't been for his friend Jihad. When Jihad got locked up, Leaf promised to take care of him for as long as he was in there. So far, Leaf had stayed true to his promise and regularly deposited $200 on Jihad's books. He didn't visit too often, but when he did, it was greatly appreciated by Jihad. Leaf was just about the only person that ever visited him. Respectfully speaking, he was all he had.

When Jihad entered the visiting room, he was directed to a booth in the back. Once inside, a pretty black chick introduced herself as Amy Tyler. She was accompanied by a smug-looking white man that seemed to be reading through some paperwork on the table. The man was so engrossed in the paperwork that he didn't even bother to look up at Jihad when he walked in.

"Take a seat, Mr. Cooper," Amy instructed him. Jihad complied, anxious to see what this was all about.

"We're going to get right down to business," Amy said, not wanting to waste any time beating around the bush. "We are with the FBI and ATF, and we feel that you may be able to help us out. In return, we are willing to help you. If we both come to an agreement, we may be able to assist each other. We believe in the exchange program, meaning we can get you out in the snap of a finger, but you have to be willing to help us with a situation we are attempting to resolve," she said.

"Look, lady, you're cute and all, but I doubt you and your boy over there have the power to get me out." Jihad sat across from them with doubt written all over his face. "I don't know if you know, but I'm in here for at least forty years."

"We are well aware of your situation, Mr. Cooper," the white man finally spoke and looked up at him.

"My man, who the fuck are you?" Jihad questioned. The man's face turned red, and even a blind person would be able to tell Jihad's question had pissed him off.

"I'm sorry," Amy interjected. "This is my associate, Adam Steinberg."

Adam cleared his throat and tucked at his shirt collar. He hated having to work deals with convicted felons. He didn't necessarily agree with the exchange program, but he didn't make the rules or the laws. His job was to enforce them, and that was always his main priority.

"As I was saying," Adam paused before continuing, "we are well aware of your situation. You're serving a fifty-year sentence for killing a man and shooting his girlfriend twice in the neck." Adam glanced down at the sheet of paper he had been reading when Jihad walked in. "Correct me if I'm wrong, but according to your statement, you shot the man and woman because they had, and I quote, 'disrespected your gangster,'" Adam said as he did his best to hide the disgust he felt inside. He felt sick to his stomach to have to do business with scum like this.

"A'ight." Jihad didn't confirm nor deny Adam's statement even though he knew the man had just retold exactly what his case was. " . . . and what's your situation?" asked Jihad.

"With all due respect, I can't share that information with you unless we have a signed agreement that you are willing to cooperate. It is classified, but I can assure you we can make good on our promise to get you released and possibly even have your sentence considered as time fully served. Do you need time to think about it, or do we have a deal, Mr. Cooper?" Amy asked while sliding a pen and paper over to him.

Jihad had a million things running through his head. He wasn't crazy about the idea of becoming like all the other niggas and bitches he knew who had turned their backs and shitted on him the second he was sentenced. As good as the offer sounded, Jihad was against any assistance or cooperation with the police. In fact, he was an antirat. He had personally killed snitches and barred them from his sight in the past. Jihad almost felt sick to his stomach at the thought of becoming a rat. Realistically, though, he knew he'd probably never get this opportunity again, and at the rate he was going in prison having to fight all the time, he most likely would end up having to do the whole fifty years his sentence called for.

Just then, almost instantly, a brilliant plan came to mind. He would sign just to get out, and then warn whoever they were onto before going on the run. He picked up the pen and signed his signature.

Guess Who's Back?

"Leaf! Get in here quick . . . You ain't gonna believe who's on the Channel Six news! Your man's just beat the system," said Sha'Ron as he stood in front of the TV tuned into the twelve o'clock news. Leaf rushed in just in time to catch the top story. They were talking about the release of a violent offender with an extensive criminal history consisting of guns, shootings, and even murders. The district attorney was preparing to speak in seconds concerning the matter.

"This is Lauren Buckman, reporting live from Graterford State Prison where Jihad Cooper is scheduled to be released in a matter of minutes. Mr. Cooper was sentenced in 2002 to forty to fifty years for the murder of a man in West Philadelphia and the shooting of the man's girlfriend. Mr. Cooper has somehow found a loophole in the criminal justice system and has used it to gain his freedom. I'm live with District Attorney Ken Abraham who will try to answer one question . . . Where did our criminal justice system go wrong?"

"Well, for one, our criminal justice system is not perfect. We deal every day with witness intimidation, statements being changed, and police corruption. Mr. Cooper's charges are not being dismissed; he's been given a new trial due to ineffective counsel. A witness who should have testified on Mr. Cooper's behalf was never mentioned in his discovery, which was a violation

of his constitutional rights. Therefore, the district attorney's office has no choice but to release Mr. Cooper on his own recognizance and give his witness a chance to testify at a new trial. No further questions at this time," said the DA while turning from the cameraman.

Thirty minutes later, Jihad walked out of the jail being escorted by two COs. Lauren Buckman rushed to him and asked a question.

"How does it feel to be released?"

"I'm just very fortunate that our criminal justice system works in everybody's favor. In this case, it was mine. My fight is far from over. Once I knock this case out, I plan to help my brothers who I left behind fight their cases as well. I want to give a shout-out to—" He was cut off midsentence before the two COs pulled him away from the media and led him to a van.

"Ain't that some shit," Leaf exclaimed. He was excited and happy to learn that his boy had gotten out. He was looking forward to seeing his boy on the outside again.

Meanwhile, across town, Jihad stood alone at a corner after being dropped off in downtown Philly. He was told someone would be picking him up, but he'd been standing there for almost half an hour and was beginning to think he'd gotten lucky and was going to be able to make his escape faster than he'd originally thought. He was about to walk away when he spotted a fine-ass Puerto Rican-looking woman walking toward him. She was wearing a long, tube top sundress. Her titties were bouncing with every step she took, and she had hips for days. Jihad immediately felt his dick start to get hard. It'd been five years since he'd had some pussy. He licked his lips and salivated just thinking about dicking this woman down. The woman walked right up to him and pulled him in to a warm embrace. Jihad put his arms around her, and she leaned in to whisper something in his ear.

"Hold my hand and walk toward the black van with the tinted windows," she instructed. Jihad didn't bother to even question her and did exactly as he was told. Whoever this woman was, she was about to get her brains fucked in that van. They walked toward the van and got in. As soon as Jihad stepped inside, all hopes of him getting laid flew right out the window. Inside the van were Amy, Adam, and an unknown agent. The fly Puerto Rican agent introduced herself as Vickie Perez. She went into her bag and pulled out a large sum of money and a belt, which he learned was fully equipped with an electronic listening device. He was given strict instructions on how to use it. He was never to remove the electrical device that was planted inside the buckle of his belt, nor was he to leave it unattended. If he did, a sensor would alert the feds, and the investigation would be over. In that instance, he would then be brought back to prison to do the remaining forty-five years out of his original fifty-year sentence. They also informed him that in the event that he was returned to prison, the agreement he signed would become public record, and they'd make sure to air it on the news so his prison and street friends would know what he'd been up to. They gave him five grand up front for him to use on any expenses he might need to further help him with their investigation.

He learned that they wanted him to help in an ongoing investigation involving Gustavo Santana. They knew that he was close friends with Gustavo's cousin Ka'Leaf Santana, and they wanted him to link back up with Ka'Leaf and get him to spill some family secrets. Jihad's heart dropped when he realized they had set him up to turn on one of his best friends. After the feds got done schooling him and warning him of what he was allowed to do and not do, they dropped him off at his mother's house.

As soon as he stepped inside, his alcoholic mother immediately stood to her feet and walked toward her son. She had seen on the news that her only son had gotten released earlier that day. She'd been expecting him for hours; not so much because she was looking forward to seeing him, but more because she was running low on cash, and she knew he'd help her out.

"Would you look what the cat dragged in?" She said it more like a statement than a question. "I hope you don't think your ass is staying here for free. You better peel me off a li'l something. I know your ass got money." She slurred her words as she put her hand out, expecting Jihad to put some bills in it. Jihad couldn't believe after five years, she was still up to the same old tricks. He was actually surprised she hadn't been kicked out of the house by now. Before he was arrested, he was the one that paid and took care of everything for her.

Damn, ain't shit changed around here, he thought to himself as he shook his head and walked past his mother, leaving her standing with her hand stretched out.

"Where you going? You need to give me some money, Jihad." He made his way upstairs toward his old bedroom. He could hear his mom's footsteps following close behind. Jihad immediately regretted listing his mother's address as his place of residence.

"Same shit, different day, huh?" asked Jihad as he turned to face her. He peeled off two twenties and put them in her hands.

"Now, that's more like it," she said before walking back downstairs and into the living room. He was ashamed of her, but still loved her dearly.

"Clean this place up and no company," he demanded before letting himself into his room. He couldn't wait to get some much-needed sleep in his own bed. He entered his room and was surprised that his mom had been doing a decent job keeping up with it. He was even more surprised that most of his clothes were still there. He lay on his bed contemplating what the fuck he got himself into. It was clear that his plan was not going to go as he intended. The feds were too advanced to be outwitted. *What the fuck have I got myself into? I done put in too much work to go down in history as a rat. Fuck this.* Remembering his secret stash spot that held his Glock 40, he quickly went to retrieve it. Jihad's thoughts were all over the place. He couldn't stop his heart from racing. The many could-haves and would-haves plagued his thoughts. With tears running down his face, he placed the gun to his temple, believing that suicide would rescue him from the extremely uncomfortable situation he put himself into. Just when he was about to pull the trigger, his mother's voice interrupted his suicide.

"Jihad! Jihad! I know you hear me, boy. Your friend Ka'Leaf is down here with some nice-looking girls."

Aw, shit, Jihad thought as he jumped up, tucking his gun in his waist. Leaf had no idea that he had just saved his friend's life. Once he walked down those steps and came in the presence of Leaf, he was overcome with guilt. He knew he would either have to warn his boy or fulfill his obligation as an informant. Deciding the best choice for him, he gathered himself together. There was no way he was going to allow Leaf to see him sweat.

When he finally arrived downstairs, he observed Leaf posted up with two dime pieces, thicker than cough syrup. Every piece of jewelry Leaf had on was infested with diamonds. He could tell by his swagger that he had gotten his weight up. Jihad walked up to his little homie to exchange hugs and shakes.

"Nigga, you got big as shit up in there. Something like the Matrix. I just came by to welcome you back home as you should be. Nobody could ever walk in your shoes, nigga, and now that you're back, it's time you reestablish yourself with us. Things changed a lot, homie, I got a lot of shit to catch you up on. Your presence with us is needed." Leaf gave his boy a pound, "But before we get into all that, I brought these two young things for you as a little welcome back gift from yours truly. Plus, I'ma have a nice check for you tonight when you come to Freeze's. So, go freshen up, wash your ass, and *get* you some ass. Enjoy yourself . . . I got you," he added before leaving his homie to take care of his business.

Ring! Ring! Ring! Trish was seconds away from reaching an orgasm, all in Gus's mouth when the ringing telephone interrupted her concentration. She angrily snatched the receiver off the cradle.

"What?" she barked, visibly upset about being disturbed.

"Yo, where Gus at?" asked Leaf, not giving a fuck about Trish or her attitude.

"Why don't you call his cell phone? This is *my* line," she snapped.

"Don't you think I already did that, smart-ass?"

"Well, if he don't answer his phone, then he's probably busy. Bosses ain't on standby, just the flunkies," said Trish while slamming the phone back down to send Leaf a clear message.

"Baby, you ain't have to say all that with your crazy ass," said Gus while cracking up laughing.

"So what? That nigga fucked up my mood. Plus, that nigga need to know his position. Now, come on, Gus, and finish sucking on this bald pussy."

After Gus put Trish to sleep with his pipe game, he hopped up in his 750 and called Leaf. After a few rings, he answered.

"Damn, nigga, I know you seen me trying to call you all fucking day, having to deal with your disrespectful-ass bitch. Slide through Freeze's real quick. I got a surprise for you."

"All right, nigga, I'll be down in a few," Gus replied before ending the call. Gus was irked at the way his cousin had just talked to him. *Who the fuck this nigga think he's talking to?* he questioned even though he already had an idea of why Leaf was talking with so much confidence all of a sudden. Gus already knew Leaf's surprise was Jihad being freed. He didn't quite understand why Leaf would think he'd be excited to see Jihad again. Jihad was Leaf's homeboy, not his. Truth be told, he had never been very fond of Jihad because he felt like Leaf always acted different when he was around. Leaf was a hotheaded nigga as it was, but whenever he was with Jihad, he got worse, and Gus didn't like that. He already felt like Jihad coming back into the picture was going to be nothing more than a headache to him. Gus was sure Jihad's presence explained where Leaf's disrespectful mouth suddenly came from.

Get the Patrón and Tell 'Em That I'm Home

Freeze's was an upscale neighborhood bar owned by a big-time drug dealer named Vic. The baddest bitches in the city attended the bar on a regular basis. Most of them came hoping to mingle and score with some of the robbers, hustlers, and ballers that threw money around as if it were hot potatoes.

When Gus entered Freeze's, Lil Wayne's hood anthem, "Money on My Mind," cranked through the state-of-the-art speakers. Gus walked through looking like a million-dollar bill. He sported an iced-out Audemars Piguet watch, True Religion jeans, and a skull shirt. The niggas he passed while walking through only had their hand shaken if they were somebody. Others were lucky to get a head nod.

When Gus approached their personal reserved table, he spotted Leaf, Sha'Ron, and Jihad surrounded by a dozen skeezers. Getting a closer look, he noticed one of them sucking Jihad's dick as he enjoyed his drink. This was common treatment for the Santanas and their associates.

"Look at this nigga here. What the fuck is up, my nigga?" said Jihad after pushing the girl away and fixing himself up. He jumped up to show Gus some love. He gripped him up and gave him one of those drunk I-love-you hugs.

"I told my nigga he family, and our arms always have and will remain open to him," Leaf stated.

"Well, you know the rule, but fuck all that business talk. Let's celebrate the nigga's release," replied Gus being clear to mention *the rule* which was: *if you brought somebody in, they were your responsibility for good or bad.*

Since Leaf was only the family's basic strongman and main shooter, he went on and explained to Gus that he wanted Jihad to come in as the second shooter. He wanted him and Jihad to be the Santanas' main security and marksmen. As much as Gus wasn't too fond of Jihad, he couldn't deny that the man had crazy shooting skills. As long as Leaf and Jihad played their position and stayed in their lane, Gus felt he was in a win-win situation. *You can never have too much security* was his justification for allowing Jihad in.

It was just a matter of time before the Santanas and their associates conquered every street in Philadelphia. With their mothers being out and moving in with the boys as soon as their two weeks at the halfway house were up, Gus was sure they were about to shut the whole game down and blow shit out of the water. Using muscle, intimidation, and hustle like a weapon, all of their hard work was going to pay off soon.

Meanwhile, Black stepping in, taking Gus under his wing, was the best thing that could have ever happened to him. Black was glad that Connie had reached out to him and asked him to look after the boys because now, all he had to do was sit back, put his feet up, and watch the money roll in from Gus's hard work. Black had money before, but with Gus now in the picture, he'd be stupid rich. The nigga had more money than he and his family could spend in a lifetime.

Black was being extra careful in making sure his prodigy believed he was in full control. He was also making sure that all of Gus's business transactions could not be traced back to him, just in case something was to go down. He loved Gus but not enough to go down with the ship if it ever started to sink. He appreciated Gus's dedication and loyalty though, so he had already decided Gus would be his predecessor when he retired, which was going to be sooner rather than later.

He was amazed at how well things had been going since he put Gus on, and he was ready to pass the torch. He had already decided that in six months he would cut his ties and hand Gus the entire operation. His days as headmaster would soon be coming to a close. He was ready and excited to retire from the game and start to enjoy the fruits of his labor.

Becoming a Star . . . (Rats)

Amy sent Jihad a message earlier in the day that he was to meet up with them at five-thirty that afternoon. The meeting's location was the parking lot at Pathmark Supermarket off of Belmont Avenue. This was Jihad's second meeting with the feds, and he was a nervous wreck. He still felt uncomfortable as hell in his new role. They expected him to give them piece by piece, detail by detail, every second he spent around Leaf or the two other Santanas.

He still had yet to figure a way out. But until then, he had to play it by ear. When he arrived in the parking lot, he parked the van where the agents awaited him. After briefly looking around the lot, Jihad cautiously exited his car and then slid in the side door of the van. He was greeted by Amy and the other agents. They appeared to be upset. Adam wasted no time informing him why.

"When are you going to help us with this investigation? Because, personally, I think you are just taking us on a ride. So far, all we've heard is you chilling with your homies, drinking, and getting your dick sucked. That's not what we got you for. You're supposed to be getting them to talk so we can get some inside information." Adam was so mad, you could see the veins on his neck and forehead. "You know what? I don't need your bullshit. This assignment is over. I'm taking your ass back to Graterford," Adam snapped before throwing the clipboard he had in his hand across the van. He stood up and placed handcuffs on Jihad before sitting him down in the seat. The agent that was driving was instructed to head to Graterford.

Jihad stayed silent throughout the entire ordeal. In a way he felt relieved to be taken back. He didn't feel right ratting on his boys and setting them up. He couldn't argue with Adam because everything he'd said was the truth. Jihad had been bullshitting. He'd been stalling for days to avoid doing what he'd signed up for.

During the first five minutes of the ride, Amy tried to talk Adam out of returning Jihad, but to no avail. He wasn't trying to hear anything. Instead, he got on his phone and talked to his supervisor.

"Yes, this is Agent Adam Steinberg. I'm just notifying you that the Santana investigation is being shut down, and the confidential informant is being returned to SCI Graterford. I'll have a briefing on your desk in the morning, sir. Thank you," he announced before disconnecting.

The reality that Jihad was heading back to prison began to set in. He closed his eyes and took deep breaths. He'd gotten a nice little taste of freedom, and he wasn't ready to give it up just yet. Shit definitely didn't go as he planned. He thought that as long as he gave them bullshit information here and there that it would buy him time to figure a way to get out of the bind he was in. But clearly, they hadn't been as patient as he thought. The situation he now had at hand was life and death. He knew if he went back and his spot got blown, he'd be beaten to death, and he wasn't trying to die on anybody's terms but his own. The reality of that was more than enough reason for him to finally react to what was going on in this moment.

"Hold up, y'all. I wasn't even given the opportunity to say what I learned. Y'all acting like this some shit I did all my life. I ain't even get a chance to adjust myself." Adam appeared unfazed by the speech, but Amy was curious to know what Jihad had learned.

"And what is it that you have learned?" she asked.

"Well, Leaf mentioned that the connect was the ol' head Black from down southwest who been moving around doing his thing for years. With that nigga backing them up, they untouchable," he revealed, feeling like a piece of shit for giving up information about his little homie to the feds. Just the mention of Black's name prompted Adam to respond to Jihad's statement, with his eyes wide open and beads of sweat trickling down his forehead.

"What Black are you referring to? Are you talking about Curtis 'Black' Campbell? Why didn't we hear any mention of his name through the piece on your belt? And how do you know Leaf was talking about the guy Black specifically?" Adam fired question after question, barely giving Jihad a chance to answer any of them.

"Everybody knows that Black has been their mothers' connect from way back in the day," Jihad explained. "From what I understand, Connie reached out to Black while she was still locked up and asked Black to look out for the Santana boys. Black put Gus on, and that's the only reason Gus been doing so good lately. You think everything they been doing was done by themselves?" Jihad paused. "C'mon, man, you know shit don't get done in Philly without that OG's blessing."

Jihad felt a little more comfortable spitting all that information after seeing Adam's reaction when he first mentioned Black's name. Jihad had no loyalties to Black, so he figured maybe he could get these motherfuckers to go after Black instead of the Santanas.

"I'm going ask you one more question and be careful the way you answer me." Adam leaned in and got right in Jihad's face. "How do we know everything you just said is the truth? We didn't hear any of this through the live feed from your belt."

"I don't know, man. This all happened when we was at Freeze's. Maybe everything got muffled because the music was blasting. I ain't no tech man. I don't know how all that electronic shit works." Jihad shrugged his shoulders. Truth be told, Jihad really didn't know much about electronic stuff, but he did know the reason why they hadn't heard any of that through the belt. When Jihad went to Freeze's with Leaf, he had grabbed a pillow from the VIP spot they were sitting at and put it over the belt in hopes that it would muffle their conversation.

Adam took in everything Jihad said, and at his request, the van got off at the first exit and parked in the driveway of a fast-food restaurant. All the agents, with the exception of the driver, got out of the van where they had an urgent meeting. Words were exchanged, situations were compromised, and phone calls were made. When the agents got back into the van, they treated Jihad with a newly discovered degree of respect.

"I'm sorry for the misunderstanding, Jihad, and I apologize for losing my patience. I'm sure that once we better prepare you for these situations, we'll work better together," said Adam with an Oscar Award–winning performance. They never had any intentions of really returning Jihad to jail. It had all been an act to get Jihad riled up and scared that he'd be getting sent back. It was strictly strategy, and it had worked like a charm.

"Jihad, we have reason to believe that the Santana boys are throwing a big welcome back party for their mothers. Do you know anything about that?" Amy asked.

"Um, yeah. They're throwing the sisters a huge party this weekend at the Taj Mahal in Atlantic City," he informed them.

"Okay, this Friday is the day they're scheduled to get out of the halfway house," Amy said as her thoughts raced. "I have an idea that, if planned out carefully, it could possibly bring you closer to Gus. With the information you just supplied us, we might be going after Black too now. I'm going to need a few days to get everything planned out. For your protection and ours, we'll meet up Friday morning and prepare you for what the next moves will be, so be well rested. You think you can handle it?" asked Amy.

"I don't have a choice, Amy. Shit done got a whole lot realer," said Jihad. When they dropped him back off at his car . . . he felt like the weight of the world was on his shoulders. His back was against the wall, and he had no idea what he was going to do to get out of the mess he had put himself in. He had a lot of shit to think about over the next few days. His life depended on it.

Now or Never

Friday afternoon, Jihad had just returned from meeting up with the agents. The plan that they had explained to him seemed suicidal and reminded him of some shit out of an action movie, but fuck it, his freedom depended on it. After going over things in his head repeatedly, he finally came to a decision about what he was going to do. Jihad was prepared to play both sides of the fence for as long as he could. After facing the reality of almost being sent back, he justified his decision to seriously cooperate with the feds as life or death. On the other hand, though, if it came down to a shoot-out between the feds and the Santanas, Jihad was willing to take a bullet and die protecting his boy Leaf. By all means necessary, Jihad wasn't going back to jail. He'd rather get put in body bag than to get put back in Graterford handcuffs.

His thoughts were interrupted by the beeping of a horn. From his bedroom window, he noticed Leaf's silver F-150 pickup truck was parked outside of his house. They were driving over to Atlantic City together. Jihad tucked the gun given to him by the feds on his hip. With all the stress and worry, he was looking forward to relieving it by partying in Atlantic City.

Connie and Consuela's welcome home party was the talk of Philly. Everyone had been looking forward to this party. Only the cream of the crop and those that had been rolling with the twins from day one were invited. Gus and Trish had been planning the party from the second they learned of the twins' premature release. Gus had given Trish unlimited access to his account and told her not to worry about any of the costs. Leaf and Sha'Ron didn't care so much about the party itself, so they focused more on taking the girls shopping for their outfits and making sure they got all glamoured up for their big day. They didn't know anything about fashion, but they enjoyed seeing the excitement in Connie and Consuela's eyes while they shopped for the perfect dress and designed their custom jewelry and got their hair and makeup done. The boys took pride in being able to treat their mother and aunt so lavishly.

Trish knew how much the twins loved diamonds so the theme of the party was "Diamonds Are Forever." The private ballroom she chose had crystal chandeliers throughout the ceiling. Each table had been decorated to look like Tiffany's signature colors. The tablecloths were turquoise and the runners were jet black. The centerpieces were silver branches placed inside glass cylinder vases. Swarovski crystals hung from the branches like whimsical icicles, and tiny crystals were scattered throughout the tables to add the perfect finishing touch.

A famous comedian by the name Mac Williams was hosting the party as well as performing a forty-five minute stand-up act. The bar was stocked with hundreds of bottles of top-shelf liquors and champagnes. There was filet mignon, lobster tails, and Cornish hens on the menu, to be accompanied with mashed potatoes and roasted vegetables.

Trish had even made sure to rent out three entire floors for the guests to stay in when the party was over. Leaf and Sha'Ron surprised the twins and rented two of the latest Rolls-Royces in their favorite colors; one black and the other white. When the two drop-top Rolls-Royces, pulled up in front of the Taj Mahal, a sudden silence came over the crowd of rowdy partygoers who came out with intentions to support and celebrate the twins' release. There was a good amount of onlookers curious to discover the identity and names of the individuals that were causing all of this commotion. As the doors to the Roll-Royces opened up, Connie and Consuela Santana stepped out looking like superstars. Wearing their favorite colors, they wore skintight Gucci dresses, Red Bottom high heel shoes, and actual princess crowns covered in a rainbow of diamonds. Their entrance alone was showstopping. Even the hustlers with major money didn't dare approach the twins in a flirtatious manner nor make advances. Everyone knew the sisters did not take disrespect lightly.

The event turned out to be a success. The musicians that performed did so with style and perfection. Impressively, they even encouraged the audience of gangsters, hustlers, and bosses to join in and sing along and keep up with their dance moves. But the night wasn't complete until the comedian did his hilarious stand-up performance. When he came out, he went right after the twins.

"What's up, party people? Everybody looking all good and rich. Thank God for cocaine and crack. Look at the twins, all thick from them jailhouse grits and potatoes," said Mac, as one of the twins gave him a playful evil stare while balling her fist up.

"Naw, I'm only fucking with you girls. Both of you look beautiful, by the way. Please don't put a hit out on me! I already fucked up, coming in this bitch without my bulletproof vest and my nine. I got to stop smoking so much weed because I done forgot to tell Black and Gus that I wasn't doing the show unless they provided metal detectors to search all these motherfucking gangsters in here." Mac went on for about an hour, leaving the crowd cracking up. His performance was one for the books.

The after-party took place at a hip-hop club called The Lounge. Leaf and Jihad led the way over while Gus and Sha'Ron followed. While parking their cars side by side, no one took notice of the caravan that looked out of place with PA plates. It circled the lot once, then came right back around. Suddenly, gunshots rang out! There was a nigga shooting a fully loaded automatic weapon from out of the sliding side door of the van, directed straight at Gus and Sha'Ron as they sat helplessly inside Gus's BMW. As if on cue, Jihad jumped from the truck squeezing shot after shot from his Glock at the would-be assassins. One of his bullets hit the shooter in the head, stopping him dead in his tracks. The van sped away as the shooter's body hung from the open sliding door.

Jihad's adrenaline was pumping as he ran over to the BMW, where Gus and Sha'Ron sat shocked and scared with minor injuries from the glass fragments.

"Yeah, nigga, I rocked that pussy. *That's* how I do. Ain't shit change . . . Y'all see how I move. Let's get the fuck up out of here," yelled Jihad with excitement, still holding the smoking gun. The entire parking lot was in a frenzy, as the would-be-partygoers ran for cover and sped out of the lot, hoping to avoid being shot. Because of the chaos, the after-party was completely shut down and everybody decided to flee the scene and make it back to Philly safely. Before exiting Atlantic City, Jihad threw the Glock over the bridge into a small channel of water below—just as the feds had instructed him to do.

Foot in the Door

"Wow, what a good job! I personally congratulate all of you. You guys were excellent and no one got hurt. Jihad did a great job as well. He followed instructions to the tee, and we were even able to recover the gun. To show my appreciation for the great job done, I'm treating everyone to a drink," said Adam, who was hardly ever satisfied with his agents enough to treat them to anything. But since they had executed their plan with precise accuracy, he wanted to reward them for their hard work. It was risky to use live ammunition, but that was the risk they were willing to take in order to give the scene a realistic approach. The Hollywood-like special effects were something straight out of the movies. The blank bullets that were left on the scene from Jihad's gun could not be identified as a blank; therefore, any reports about the incident would be official and realistic as well.

Everyone grabbed their keys and got ready to leave the office and go to the bar a few blocks down. Just as Amy reached the front office door, she heard Adam call out her name. She stopped and waited for him to catch up.

"Amy, that was great idea on your part, by the way. None of this would have been possible if it hadn't been for you planning all of this out." Adam praised her, "Believe me, I'm going to make sure the department knows you've been the brains behind this entire operation. To be honest with you, they originally assigned me to work with you on this case because they didn't think you could do it on your own. But you sure as hell are proving them wrong," Adam admitted.

"Thanks, Adam," was all Amy could say. Hearing all of this was bittersweet. It felt great to be commended by Adam. Adam was a highly respected senior officer that had been in the force for over fifteen years. To have him pay her such a compliment meant the world to her. On the other hand, she was disappointed to hear that the department didn't have much hopes for her when they put her on this case. Adam sensed her mixed emotions and decided to give her a few more words of encouragement.

"Hey, listen." He grabbed her by the shoulders and looked directly into her eyes. "Don't take what I just said personal. They treat all rookies like that in the beginning. You just keep proving them wrong." Having said that, he winked and released her shoulders, "Now, let's go catch up with everyone before there's no beer left at the bar."

Amy chuckled and decided to do exactly what Adam had just advised her.

When You Gamble with Safety, You Bet Your Life

The following day, Gus paced the floor of his living room trying to figure out who was responsible for the attempted hit. He and Trish had been arguing all night about the entire situation, and she was scared she was going to lose him. Her concerns were understandable, but she just chose the wrong time to express them. Gus's nerves were shot from the near-death experience. It was enough reason to want tighter security around himself. Although they were out celebrating, Leaf should never have let his guard down. If it wasn't for Jihad's fast thinking and reaction, he might have been killed last night. His new outlook on life was on a higher level, as was his greater degree of respect for Jihad. He witnessed Jihad kill for him, and for that, he was grateful. Leaf was supposed to have his back, but last night, Leaf looked out for himself. Gus no longer felt comfortable with Leaf, and for that reason, he was going to offer Jihad the position as his personal enforcer.

Jihad wasn't shocked when Gus called his phone the following morning after the shooting. He sounded real nervous, stating that he wanted to meet up with him immediately. This was just what the feds had predicted.

Before pulling up to Jihad's house, Gus called and told him that he was in a black Grand Prix. After the shooting, he decided to put all of his cars up and get a rental.

As soon as he pulled up and Jihad got inside, he noticed Gus appeared to be scared and worried. It was as if he was expecting someone to jump out of nowhere and shoot him. They rode in silence for a few moments before Gus addressed him.

"Jihad, that was good looking, my nigga. You saved my life, and I'm forever indebted to you. The way you reacted was quick and without a second thought. I need that blanket of security at all times. In this business, you can never be too careful. The type of moves I'm making require constant observation of my surroundings. So, I'm prepared to give you two hundred grand right now and twenty-five stacks a month, if you agree to be that extra assurance I need. The only condition I make is that you move into my crib and be prepared to throw down at anytime, anywhere, or anyplace. What you say, my nigga?" he asked.

"Nigga, you like family. It ain't even about the money, Gus. It's about riding for the cause, homie. I got your back," responded Jihad, as he sealed the deal with a handshake.

"I know it ain't even about the paper, but since I'ma require a lot of your time and undivided attention, I insist," said Gus while reaching into the backseat of the car and retrieving a large Coach bag. He placed it on Jihad's lap. There was no protesting.

"I'm hungry as shit. You wanna slide past Ace's Diner?" asked Gus, feeling unstoppable now that he had Jihad as his top enforcer.

"Yeah, I'm all for it. I ain't had nothing to eat since last night at the party," Jihad remarked.

When the two entered Ace's, they were given special treatment and fast service, as usual. Gus was well known at most restaurants throughout the city, and he was known to be a heavy tipper. While waiting on their breakfast, which consisted of beef bacon, cheese eggs, toasted bread, and home fries, Jihad couldn't believe who he bumped into. His ex-girlfriend, Cristina, was sitting at a nearby table with some dusty-looking nigga, sporting some Old Navy-looking shit. When she spotted him sitting with Gus, she acted like she was by herself and she hadn't just been holding the next nigga's hand.

"Oh my God . . . Is that Jihad? Hey, boy, when the fuck you get out of jail?" Cristina asked after running up on Jihad, hugging him as if they were still a couple.

"Excuse me for a second, homie. Bring your ass over here, bitch," said Jihad, stepping away from the table and pulling Cristina over toward the restrooms. Seeing that the restroom area was empty and out of view of the employees and customers, he pushed her into the men's room.

"Bitch, I should blow your head off. Not only did your funky ass leave me, but you took my little bit of money and left me dry. Now that you see me back out here, you acting like we supposed to be cool or something. Fuck you!"

"Jihad, all I knew was you, and when you left me, I was all alone. I started stripping and taking pills to stop myself from thinking about you. And, I didn't spend your money. Somebody broke into my house and stole it. I miss you, Daddy, and I miss the taste of that chocolate dick," said Cristina while stealing a sneak touch, making his dick get hard almost instantly. Seeing that her touch still held power, she dropped to her knees, unbuckled his pants, and started eating that dick up like she invented blow jobs. She slurped, sucked, and swallowed every drop of him. She was hoping that the mean head game would earn her position back.

Once she was done putting that jaw to work, Jihad's dick was still rock hard, and now he wanted to fuck. He quickly snatched her up to her feet and began pulling her jeans and panties down in one swift motion. He bent her over the sink forcefully. While she was expecting it in her pussy, he took a different approach and stuck his dick right up her asshole without mercy. He beat it up until she cried. When he was done, he wiped his shitty, bloody dick off on the back of her shirt as she stood there bent over in excruciating pain. In a further attempt to humiliate her, he pulled out a twenty-dollar bill and some ones and threw them at her before she stood up and tried to gather herself together.

"Bitch, I bet the next time you shit on a nigga like me, you going to remember to wipe your ass afterward. I kept you dressed in the finest and treated you like a queen. As soon as the clouds started showing, you ran and took cover. Then when it started raining, you left me out there by myself. When the storm came, you completely abandoned me. Well, guess what, bitch? The sun is out shining again. You should have had some patience, but you chose to keep me in the dark, and now you ain't shit to me. If my mouth wasn't dry, I'd spit in your face," replied Jihad before turning his back on her.

When he pushed the door to exit, he got a slight bit of resistance. So, he kicked it as hard as he could, only to see Cristina's little dusty nigga flying backward. The chump must've heard the whole thing and didn't even try to intervene. Jihad pulled the coward into the bathroom as well.

"What the fuck . . . You spying on me, nigga? I tell you what. Since you want to disrespect me, you going to take your tire-changing-looking ass outside and scrub the white walls on that Grand Prix, or else I'ma empty my clip out on your chest. Matter of fact, just in case you try to leave without cleaning my tires, give me your license so I can see where you lay your head up at night. Try to run and I'm gonna pay you a visit at home. Is that understood, nigga? Now, bring your raggedy ass on," said Jihad as the scared dusty nigga followed close behind him. Gus couldn't believe what he had just seen. He couldn't help but to laugh to himself at how crazy Jihad really was.

Jihad went to the waitress that had served them and told her he would pay her a hundred dollars for a bucket with hot water and a rag. She complied without hesitation. When she came back to the table with his request, he pointed to the bucket, prompting Christina's new boyfriend to pick it up without argument. Cristina watched on in embarrassment. But she knew that Jihad would have killed both of them without hesitation.

When they finished their breakfast and stepped outside, they were surprised to see that the white walls were so clean, the tires looked brand new. Gus was so amazed he gave the nigga a fifty-dollar tip. Jihad got back into the car cracking up laughing. Before they pulled off, Cristina ran out of Ace's crying and screaming how sorry she was. In return, Jihad wrote his number on a five-dollar bill and tossed it out the window.

"You a five-dollar ho, bitch, and your value is less than this bum-ass nigga you with. Whenever he want to clean some more tires, give me a call," Jihad said as they sped off. He didn't bother to look back.

Take 'Em to School

Later that evening, Gus made several attempts to contact Leaf, to no avail. Hours later, he finally returned the call.

"Yo, what's up, cuz? Why you blowing my phone up when for real for real, you don't fuck with me like that no more?" asked Leaf while inhaling deep tokes of Purple Haze into his lungs.

"Come on, nigga, we family. Go ahead with all that high shit. I need to holler at you and Sha'Ron later on tonight, so meet me down Freeze's around ten. Cool?"

"Yeah, that's cool. I'm supposed to pick up Sha'Ron in a few hours, so we'll be there." Shortly after ending the brief phone conversation with Leaf, his mother and Trish returned home clutching shopping bags from the mall. Trish had calmed down a great deal since Gus had moved in almost a month ago. Gus had spoken to his cousins and told them that he planned on moving in with Trish when Connie and Consuela came home. He figured it would work out better if his mother came and stayed with him and Trish for a couple of months until she was ready to get her own place; and he also thought it'd be good for Consuela to stay with her two sons in their home. Sha'Ron and Leaf both agreed, and so far, everything was working out well. Trish loved having Gus and Connie live with her. What she wasn't loving at this time was having Jihad come to live with them. There was something about him that she didn't like. He'd been living there for two weeks now, and she got a funny feeling sometimes when he was around. Nonetheless, he had agreed and proven to protect her man with his life, so that brought her some comfort. To add to that, his reputation of being a cold-blooded loyal killer outweighed any bad vibes she felt.

"Hey, baby, wait until you see what I got you. But, let me holler at you in the other room about something personal," said Connie while putting her arm around her son and guiding him into the living room, where she blasted the stereo to avoid anyone hearing what she had to tell him.

"Baby boy, I'm behind you all the way in any decision you make. But the streets is talking and watching to see how you're going to respond to the Atlantic City incident. You have to do two things . . . shut them up and show them who runs this motherfucking city. I know you don't know who is responsible for the hit, so therefore, you go at all possibilities . . . competition, rivals, and any motherfucker who looked at you wrong. But you got that nigga Jihad now. Pull your strings and work him like a puppet. Make me feel better about this situation, understood?" instructed Connie, schooling and reminding her son how he got to the top and how to remain there.

"You right, Mom. Let me fix this. I know exactly how to handle it," he guaranteed her.

There was no mystery that Connie was the real boss behind the Santana family, and always had been. Even after she and her sister were locked up, she still ran the family business from behind the scenes. Since the day Gus was born, she'd been breeding him to be a hustler and leader. It paid off big time after their incarceration, when Gus stepped up to the plate and proved he could carry the family name. This allowed the twins to remain in the background while their boys ran the show. It took sweat, blood, and tears to build the family to its current status so it would not be jeopardized for anything or anybody.

A Thug Changes . . . Love Changes . . . and Family Become Strangers

Later that night down at Freeze's, Gus and Jihad sat at the table throwing back shots of Patrón while enjoying the view of several thick bitches who stood in front of their VIP table. They were hoping for some sort of acknowledgment, such as, *Let me buy you a drink; You want to come home with me;* or *Let me take you out.* They just sat back laughing at the females, knowing that they could have any one of them with the snap of a finger.

A little after ten, Leaf and Sha'Ron walked through the door looking like superstars. If money could walk and talk, it would look like these two niggas. As the two approached the table, they were stopped over a dozen times by associates and groupie bitches. The chicks knew that if they had a chance at any of the crew, more than likely it would be Leaf or Sha'Ron, so they flocked around them with desperation. After about twenty minutes, the brothers finally made their way back to join Gus and Jihad. As soon as they sat down, Gus wasted no time addressing the issue.

"Since the other night's attempt on my life, I have made some adjustments. From now on, Jihad is going to be my personal enforcer. So, Leaf, I'm gonna need you to fall back from being security and start looking into who the fuck was responsible for the shoot-out at Atlantic City. If I was you, I'd start by calling guests and see if they say anything suspicious or any weird shit at all. You dig?" Gus tried to sound nonchalant, but he knew that Leaf was going to be upset over the sudden changes.

"Yeah? Oh yeah? That's how niggas do, huh? First of all, who the fuck do you think you are making decisions without checking with me and my brother first? I thought we do shit together as a family. And, nigga, you better remember who the gun of this family is. As a matter of fact, fuck both you niggas. I don't need any of you. Me and my little brother going to start doing our own thing. Ever since you started fucking with that old head Black, you changed up on everybody. You act like you and Black is the be-all and end-all gangsters in Philly. That motherfucker swear he gangsta, but that nigga ran as soon as he heard those shots at the party. So you know what? Fuck you and your new changes. Come on, Sha'Ron, we out," snapped Leaf, putting Sha'Ron in the middle of yet another disagreement with Gus.

"Man, y'all niggas always tripping about every little thing. Don't put me in this shit. Excuse me, I'ma get me a drink," said Sha'Ron, getting up and walking away from the table as Leaf followed behind him.

"Man, fuck that nigga. He'll get over it. The nigga expect me to continue trusting my life in his hands when a nigga almost let somebody blow my fucking head off. Hell no! Come on, Jihad, we got some shit to take care of anyway," added Gus before he downed the last of the Patrón left in his cup.

Ten minutes later, the Grand Prix slowly drove past Forty-ninth Street, where a small crowd formed around a dice game. Gus had several run-ins with the nigga that controlled the block, and after several demands, he had yet to comply and start buying coke from the Santanas. On one or more occasions, the two had heated words and friction where serious threats were made. Tonight, Gus planned to cash in on him. He parked around the corner from Forty-ninth Street, popped the trunk, and went to retrieve the AK-47 he kept concealed there. When he got back into the car with it, Jihad gave him a confused look.

"Let's go. We about to ride on these niggas. Here, take this chopper, nigga," said Gus as he passed the AK-47 to Jihad.

Before Jihad could think the situation out, they were already driving down Forty-ninth Street. Gus opened up the sunroof, then gave Jihad "the look." When they were right up on the crowd, he gave him the order to start shooting. Left with no choice, Jihad came from out of the sunroof and let the powerful assault rifle burst round after round into the unsuspecting crowd of gamblers. The shots either missed their intended targets or hit them below the waist. Jihad was a skilled shooter with almost any weapon, and if he wanted to, he could have murdered the entire crowd and still had ammunition left in his clip, when all was said and done. After fleeing the scene, they drove straight to the car rental fleet and switched cars. They traded it in for a Dodge Charger this time.

Gangsta's Gone Wild

"We got to pull him out immediately. He just committed over twenty offenses. The Atlantic City shit was one thing and no one got hurt. We have a violent criminal-turned-confidential informant acting on his own. Now, he's shooting live ammunition and injuring people. This shit's going too far, and I'm not losing my job or going to jail because we are knowingly allowing criminal activities in our investigation," exclaimed Amy, devastated after hearing the shooting through the transmitter inside of Jihad's belt. Adam stood there for a few seconds just staring at her, trying to find the right words to say. After a few moments of silence, he found them.

"Amy, I think you have the potential to be a great agent, but you have to learn that the job has to be done by any means necessary. I've been supervising agents for over fifteen years. I have earned medals, references, and job offerings, from government officials to presidents. The men and women I work with are successful professionals; and I can assure you, they are the best. You see, one thing about the federal government is, they train you in the academy on how to survive under the rules and regulations. I teach you how to work and get the best results. While you're on my team, Amy, you will back up your fellow agents until the end. And, one thing I promise you is we will not lose. Now, I need you to take control of your emotions and keep them in check. Is that understood?" Adam lectured Amy, revealing to her the method under which the feds operated.

"Yes, sir. I see it's all one big chess game, and the pawns are sacrificed to get the king," she replied with a better understanding of how things worked.

"Now you are getting the picture," said Adam with a smile.

Thirty-one, thirty-two, thirty-three bricks and $700,000. Leaf had just spent the last hour gathering all the drugs and cash he had in his safe. He felt hurt, mad, and betrayed by his cousin. What people didn't realize was that Leaf was a sensitive nigga and took shit to heart very easily. He couldn't believe that Gus had made such a crucial decision without going over it with him first. Especially when it applied to his own position. It made him feel like he was dispensable and of no importance to the family business. Seeing how Gus had just tossed him to the side like that, he was now determined to build his own empire.

You ain't the only nigga with heart and courage, cuz. I'm gonna do this shit better than you ever did, Leaf thought to himself. To conquer the streets the way he wanted to, first, he needed to gather a vicious team behind him who would acknowledge him as the gangster and boss he was, and remain loyal soldiers at all times. He had just the niggas in mind.

I Can Do Better on My Own

Leaf pulled up in his F-150 truck in front of Sygon Projects in South Philly. He was in search of two certified killers by the name of EZ and Ikeal. They had met in the county lockup a few years back. They were all fighting serious cases and weren't granted bail so they were stuck in there until their hearings. Eventually, they got cool and started to walk the yard together. They gained victories in their cases and were freed around the same time. They invited each other to their hoods and promised to link up when the time was right. That time had come. The crowd of young niggas hugging the block suddenly stopped when Leaf's unfamiliar truck sat in front of their projects, as if he were the police or rivals. They started reaching for guns and huddling up. Leaf rolled the window down before they started shooting.

"Ain't no need to get it heated. I'm looking for EZ and Ikeal," he announced firmly.

"Who the fuck is you?" asked one of the scruffy-looking young bucks.

"Leaf," he paused for a second, "Ka'Leaf Santana." He felt a little hesitant about screaming his last name out. He was really wanting to start his new identity without using the family name. The guys acted unfazed when they heard his full government name. If his name rang a bell at all, it didn't seem like it. One of them got on the phone.

Leaf stayed in the same spot and rolled his window back up. He was not going anywhere until he found these two niggas. He knew that eventually he would spot them down here. As he sat back and sparked his Dutch, two cars pulled up and boxed him in the parking lot. At least five niggas jumped out of each car, heavily armed. Leaf picked up his .40 cal, ready for whatever. Suddenly, Leaf recognized Ikeal's voice and started shouting his name.

"Ikeal, it's me, Leaf. What the fuck is good?" said Leaf as he ducked down in his seat.

"Aw, shit, Leaf. What the fuck is wrong with you coming down here talking 'bout you looking for niggas, with all the drama we got going on down here? Come the fuck out here, you crazy-ass nigga," said Ikeal before he ordered his team to disperse. When Leaf climbed out of the truck, he was greeted by Ikeal and EZ. They expressed their love and respect for one another through handshakes and an extended hug.

"Man, y'all niggas is shot the fuck out. Didn't the young niggas say it was me? I thought it was about to go down," said Leaf, shaken up a little about the miscommunication.

"What? You told them young niggas over there who you were?" asked Ikeal with a confused look on his face.

"Yeah, I told them niggas my whole name," Leaf responded.

Ikeal confronted the little niggas and asked if it was true that Leaf addressed his name. When they said they hadn't heard him, EZ and Ikeal started to beat the young niggas to the ground.

"Y'all motherfuckers need to listen and pay attention to shit that gets said. This nigga almost got shot up because y'all niggas wasn't keeping your ears open," EZ yelled in between landing kicks and punches. "Now, fight back and defend yourselves," he instructed them. The little niggas fought back even though they got their asses whipped and knew they couldn't win. This was true soldier shit and just the type of discipline that Leaf needed on his team.

After Leaf shared his plans and goals for locking the city down, EZ and Ikeal were all for it. They had actually been waiting for an opportunity to come along where they could start making real moves and seeing some nice paper. Ikeal and EZ had over 75 guns and 30 soldiers that were ready to shoot, kill, and die for the cause. Their plans would take a few weeks to be put into action, and Leaf was anxious and excited to unleash his wolves. When you had a team of niggas with nothing to lose but their minds, time, and lives, nothing could stop them. Gus had no idea that he was in for a rude awakening.

We Got 99 Problems

"Consuela, I don't know what's up with these boys, but it ain't a good look right now," Connie spoke to her sister while they sat in a Jacuzzi at LA Fitness. "Trish told me Gus and Leaf had a big falling out. I been calling Leaf for two days and his little behind ain't been answering or returning my calls. The word on the streets is he talking about going his separate way and doing his own thing. You already know we can't allow that, so we need to intervene fast before this thing gets blown out of proportion."

"Goddamn that hotheaded son of mine." Consuela sucked her teeth and punched the water out of frustration. "And I bet you poor Sha'Ron is caught up in the middle of this bullshit like usual. I'm calling a family meeting tonight, and everyone that bears the last name Santana better be present, with *no* exceptions," Consuela stated, no longer feeling capable of relaxing in the Jacuzzi with her sister.

"These niggas don't know that we're responsible for all their fuckups. We need to get to the bottom of things before shit goes left or we'll have to tell Black to discontinue all business arrangements. If these boys keep fucking around, we're going to have a major war on our hands," Connie exclaimed thinking of the worst-case scenario.

Later on that evening, everyone but Leaf was in attendance for the meeting. His phone was disconnected, and no one knew how to get in contact with him. Sha'Ron and Gus had driven around to his favorite spots and asked around if anyone had seen or spoken to Leaf, but he was nowhere to be found. With or without him, the meeting was still to take place and any discussions and decisions made tonight were final. Leaf going ghost on them automatically took him out of having a say in whatever actions the Santana family took from here on out. Consuela was hurt that her son had deliberately distanced himself from them without even talking to her first, but there was too much at stake for her to give him time to come to his senses. If only Leaf had known what his moves would lead to, he would have come kicking the door down to be present at this meeting.

Connie yelled for everyone to take a seat at the dining room table. When Trish and Jihad went to grab a chair, she raised her hand and motioned toward them.

"I'm sorry but this meeting is family only. Y'all can't be here for this," Connie stated as she stared coldly at the two standing there with disappointment on their faces. Jihad really didn't give a fuck because he was going to use the time to go outside, smoke a cigarette, and contact the agents. But, Trish, on the other hand, was pissed. She flew up the steps and slammed the door so hard the house shook.

"That was messed up, Ma. You know Trish is practically family." Gus tried to stand up for his girl.

"Practically family don't mean she *family*," Connie snapped at her son and made sure to put extra emphasis on the word "family." "See, that's the problem with you boys. Y'all running around these streets bringing everybody into the family circle like it ain't shit. I love Trish and all, but at the end of the day, she doesn't carry the family name."

"That's right," Consuela agreed with her twin. "When did it become okay to bring any nigga off the street into the family business? You two better shape up and get things under control real quick. Connie and I sacrificed a lot to keep this family on top. Now, y'all niggas is telling me all our hard work and effort is over because, Gus, *you* decided to make Jihad head of security over Leaf? Don't get me wrong. I don't think you putting Leaf to a new position is a legit reason for Leaf to say fuck the family, but, Gus, it was a little messed up of you to make a big decision on your own like that. That was something you should have called a family meeting for. Now, I know my son, and I believe the shit with Leaf is deeper than just being taken off of security."

Gus and Sha'Ron sat in their seats listening to every word being said. They didn't dare try to speak and interrupt their mothers.

"Consuela and I both chose you, Gus, to lead the family's business during our absence . . . Not because you're the oldest, but because you've always been a thinker and showed leadership skills since you were a little boy." Connie looked at her only son. "You've done a hell of a job keeping things going while we were locked up, son. You've done such a good job that me and your aunt would like to stay behind the scenes and let things continue as they've been. Sha'Ron, with your brother being gone for now, I want to see you step it up and stand next to Gus. You need to be his right-hand man. I can only hope that Leaf doesn't go and do something stupid. We don't turn our back against our own, but don't let your guard down, and be ready for anything. I hope to God I'm wrong, but I have a bad feeling in the pit of my stomach that Leaf's up to no good," Connie said as she looked at the boys with worry displayed all over her face.

"I hate to say it, but I've had the same feeling since last night," Consuela admitted. "I love my son, but a mother's heart always senses when something's not right," she said as she placed her hand over her chest.

"You really think he'd turn on us, Ma?" Sha'Ron said, now feeling the weight of the conversation.

"I sure hope not," Consuela replied. She couldn't imagine having to go against her firstborn son. And if things came down to that, she wasn't even sure she'd have the heart to do it.

"All right, boys, this meeting is over." Connie wrapped everything up.

Sha'Ron rushed out of the house. He needed a drink to process everything that was said during the meeting. He couldn't fathom the idea that his brother would turn his back on them, and he felt the pressure to step his game up and stand next to his cousin. He needed a drink to calm his nerves. He got in his car and drove straight to Freeze's.

While the meeting had taken place, Jihad used the opportunity to contact Amy and smoke a Newport. He had her number memorized and always erased the record of the phone number to avoid ever being found out by someone. Amy answered on the first ring as if she was expecting him.

"Jihad, where the hell have you been? You should have contacted us. I know about some of the things that are going on, and I understand you did the best you could do under the circumstances, but it's time for another briefing. Is that possible for tomorrow?" she asked, anxious to meet up with him to get answers and understanding of the situation.

"Listen, do you remember the little bad Spanish agent named Vickie? Have her on standby tomorrow and call my phone around noon. Cool?" asked Jihad as he cautiously looked around to make sure no one was listening. Playing both sides was becoming like a game to him. He was really starting to feel like he was two different people.

When he was working with Gus, he was 100 percent dedicated to the cause. And when it was time for him to turn over information, he liked the feeling of being needed in the investigation. Jihad was so deep into his shit that he no longer felt any guilt or confusion. When he was with the Santanas, he was head of security, and when he spoke or met with the feds, he was an informant. It was almost as if Jihad had developed multiple personality disorder.

"Twelve o'clock. Be safe and keep your ears open," replied Amy.

Jihad finished his cigarette, then headed back inside where he ran into Connie, pouring herself a drink from the dining room bar.

"Where'd everybody go?" he asked her.

"Beats me. Meeting finished and everybody spread out like wildfire." Connie shrugged her shoulders. She looked him up and down and continued to stare at him as if she were trying to read his mind. He returned the look and smiled before going into the living room, where he surfed through the thousands of channels that were installed via satellite. When Connie came into the living room, she sat next to him and snatched the remote control and began changing channels. Jihad just continued to smirk, thinking to himself how crazy she was. He found it amusing.

"What . . . You find something funny, nigga? I don't like your sneaky-looking ass, so just sit there and act like I ain't even here," said Connie as she sipped her drink and put on her favorite Spike Lee movie, *She Hate Me*. Jihad got up and poured himself a drink as well. When he returned back, Connie was stretched out across the entire sofa, clearly stating that she didn't want him sitting with her. He shook his head, and then walked over to the La-Z-Boy where he adjusted it to his comfort. A few minutes into the movie, Consuela came out of the kitchen and announced she was leaving. Connie encouraged her to keep trying to get a hold of Leaf and talk some sense into him.

Upstairs, Gus was trying to comfort Trish. Her feelings were hurt because of the way Connie treated her as if she couldn't be trusted. With the close relationship she and Connie had, Trish had been under the impression that Connie loved her like a daughter. Trish was disappointed at Gus as well for allowing his mother to leave her out of the meeting. When Gus tried to touch her, she nudged his hand off of her and turned her back on him, which hurt his feelings. He hated to see Trish like this and was tired of their current status. He wanted more.

Standing up from the bed, he walked over to the other side so he could come face-to-face with Trish. Her face had dried streaks from tears running down her cheeks and eyes. Gus was ready to change that. He had heard what his mother said about Trish not having the family name, and he was ready to turn that around. He dropped to his knee and firmly grabbed hold of her hand. Staring into her puffy eyes, he expressed his feelings.

"Trish, no one has ever given me the feeling of acceptance and completion that you have given me. Your beauty is represented beyond just your looks; your heart is beautiful. I have grown to love so many things about you . . . your character, your style, and your personality. You make me happy, and for that I want to spend the rest of my life with you. So, Trish, would you marry me?" asked Gus with tears in his eyes.

"Oh my God, Gus. That was the sweetest thing anybody ever told me. Yes, I'll marry you, baby. Now, come here," exclaimed Trish, as she cried her heart out while tightly holding on to him. They began kissing each other passionately.

"This isn't the way I wanted to propose, and I promise I'm gonna have the perfect ring for you," Gus said as he brought her face up so they could stare into each other's eyes. "I love you," he said before placing a soft, tender kiss on her forehead.

"I love you too, baby."

"Let's go out and celebrate," Gus exclaimed as he pulled Trish by the hand and rushed with her downstairs.

"Ma, we're going out," he yelled out as he and Trish flew past Connie and Jihad in the living room and left.

"Well, looks like we have the house all to ourselves," Connie stated the obvious.

She changed the channel and put a different movie on. Jihad had no idea what the name of the movie was, but there were a lot of explicit sex scenes. He was shocked when Connie placed her hand in her pants and began playing with herself right in front of him, instantly arousing him. Jihad tried not to pay attention to her, afraid where things might lead. But the more she played with it, the more he watched. Once they eventually made eye contact, it was on and popping. Connie took her hand out of her pants and sucked the juices off her fingers as if to say, *this is how I'd suck your dick.* Jihad was paralyzed with shock and fear. As bad as he wanted to fuck her brains out, he couldn't move or react. Instead, he sat there licking and biting his lower lip.

Connie, being the control freak she was, had no problem taking the lead. She stood up and removed her pants, exposing her clean-shaved pink diamond. She slowly walked over to the La-Z-Boy where Jihad sat in disbelief. With her right hand, she grabbed the seat adjuster and leaned it all the way back. Afterward, she climbed over on top of him and mounted her pussy on his mouth, giving him something to feast on. With his full wet lips, he was able to manipulate her clit to be fully exposed, as he teased it, licked circles around it, and sucked it like it had never been sucked. The pleasure made her scream at the top of her lungs. Fearing that someone would hear her loud moans, he forcefully flipped her over and placed his hand over her mouth and continued giving that pussy a tongue-lashing. Now that he had full control of the situation, he stood up and picked Connie's body up into the air. Quickly pulling his dick out, he used the position to gain full access to the deepest dimension of her insides. She held on to his shoulders for dear life as he took advantage of her wet tightness. His strokes were long and touched areas of her body that had never been touched before. The harder he pumped, the louder she got. Once again becoming aware of where they were, he laid her back down on the floor and allowed her to bite down on his chest in order to muffle her screams. The pain and pleasure combined brought about multiple orgasms for Connie, and an explosive one for Jihad. It took a few minutes for them to regain composure and clean themselves up. Neither could believe what just happened between them. But there was not one regret.

What a Night Can Do

The following morning, Gus woke up in a good mood. He walked around the house singing and carrying on as if he didn't have a worry in the world. Trish seemed to be in a good mood also. She cooked breakfast for the entire household. While eating, everyone seemed happy. Connie was curious to know what the sudden happiness was all about. She hated to be in the dark about anything concerning her family, especially if it pertained to her son.

"What you so happy about, boy? I mean, Gus," Connie asked, switching her words up at the last minute for a more direct approach. When she said boy, Jihad must have thought she was talking to him because he turned redder than a fox.

"Oh, that's because Gus proposed to me last night. It was so special! We're getting married in two weeks!" interrupted Trish, answering for him. Connie gave them a funny look at first, and then eventually gave her congratulations.

Shortly after breakfast, Gus and Jihad were en route to the King of Prussia Mall to meet up with Black. He'd offered to accompany them to Tiffany's Jewelry Store where a diamond specialist was to help them choose the best quality diamond that he had to offer. Gus wanted his wife-to-be to have the best, regardless of the amount of money needed to ensure it. Jihad hadn't said anything during the ride. It appeared as if he had a lot on his mind, so Gus inquired.

"What's up, nigga? You cool? My ol' head, Black, been wanting to meet up with you since that Atlantic City incident. Do you know him?" asked Gus. Jihad was nervous because he had fucked Gus's mother, and he knew he had to meet up with the agents soon.

"Nah, I'm cool. I'm just waiting on this little Rican bitch to get at me. She be fronting on that pussy since I been home, but she supposed to get at me today," he announced.

"Well, look, nigga, I ain't going to hold you up. But at least wait until you meet the ol' head, then you can drive the Charger to go take care of your business. I'll get a ride back with Black. I know you need some pussy after doing them couple of years," added Gus.

If only he knew the pussy he'd gotten last night.

When they arrived at the mall, Black was waiting in the parking lot in a blue throwback 850 BMW. When they exited the car, Gus formally introduced Jihad to Black.

"Jihad, this is my mentor and ol' head, Black. Black, this is my man, Jihad, who I been telling you about," said Gus as the two men exchanged handshakes. All three then entered the mall. Once inside, they went straight up the escalator to the third floor where the jewelry store was. Upon entering, they were immediately acknowledged by the store's manager who announced to the few customers inside that in five minutes, the store would be closing down for a private client. After the customers left, the owner put a *Temporarily Closed* sign on the window. He was then able to give them his full, undivided attention.

"Mr. Campbell, it's always a pleasure to accommodate you. I thank you for choosing to do business with me. Your business is very well appreciated." The jeweler then turned toward Gus and Jihad to introduce himself to them. "Gentlemen, my name is Phil Edin, and I welcome you two gentlemen as guests of Mr. Campbell. I assure you that you will receive the same accommodations and hospitality as he," said Mr. Edin.

"Now, how may I assist you gentlemen here today?" he asked.

"I just proposed to my girl last night, and I need a ring to show for it. I'd like a one-of-a-kind ring because that's exactly what my fiancée is," Gus stated proudly.

While Edin was showing the men the diamond display which featured red, yellow, and green sapphire stones, complemented with platinum and VVS cuts that were brighter than the flash of a camera, Jihad was on the phone with Vickie, speaking in code that was designed to throw off anybody who was listening.

"Damn, where the fuck you been at? You been fronting like a motherfucker. You trying to get at me or what? I'm in the King of Prussia Mall right now. I can shoot up to Victoria's Secret, grab you a gift, and be at your crib in twenty minutes. So, what's it going to be?" asked Jihad, speaking in code with so much comfort and perfection, one would have thought he'd been an informant all his life.

"Okay, Jihad, I'm assuming you're trying to tell me you can only get away for a period of time, so let's hurry up and meet at the Pathmark on Belmont. How long do you suppose we'll be able to meet up for?" asked Vickie.

"As long as that pussy can stay wet. I'll probably stay in that thing for an hour or so. I'm on my way," said Jihad. Gus smiled at him before passing him the keys to the Charger. He'd overheard the entire conversation and had no idea that it really had nothing to do with meeting up for sex. After shaking hands with Black, Jihad was soon pushing the Charger back down 76. When he arrived in Pathmark's parking lot, he noticed the agents parked in their usual A-team-looking van. Finding a close parking space, he cautiously exited the car and proceeded to the van.

Once inside, Jihad was met by Adam, Amy, and an unfamiliar man who introduced himself as Special Supervising Agent Gary Shutz.

"Mr. Cooper, first and foremost, I'd like to thank and congratulate you on the hell of a job you're doing assisting us in this investigation. Now, before we continue, I need to clear up a few things. A little while back, you and Gus were at a bar meeting up with Sha'Ron and Leaf when an argument ensued. The last transmission we were able to get from the wiretap was a static version of you and Gus leaving the bar. After that, all transmissions went dead and took us hours to restore with the technical difficulties. Now when this happens, I have to fill out a ton of paperwork that I don't have the time or patience for, and I personally think the policy is bullshit. So unless some type of murder, kidnapping, or other sick shit happened, it's really no biggie if I just write, during transmission failures, nothing of importance happened. Is that cool, Jihad?" asked Gary, using manipulation in order to save their own asses. See, Gary fed Jihad a bunch of bullshit about having technical difficulties. The fed's equipment was state of the art and always kept up to date, so for them to experience any technical difficulties were either rare or unheard of. In fact, the only reason the feds had created this bogus story was because they were aware of the shooting which Jihad took part in, and they were left with two choices. Either they were to ignore it and destroy any record of it, or they'd acknowledge it, in which case they'd have to arrest Jihad and shut their investigation down. No one was seriously hurt, so in this situation, they chose to ignore it. Now all they had to do was get Jihad to sign the statement indicating that nothing of importance happened after he and Gus left the bar.

Jihad sat there with a confused look on his face as he tried to analyze what was going on. He knew what direction they were heading with all the talk about their transmissions failing coincidently, right before he and Gus went and shot up Forty-ninth Street. It was becoming clearer to him exactly how the feds operated. He was slowly learning that the feds were just as dirty and ruthless as the streets, except they had the law on their side, and how they were going after Black and the Santanas by all means necessary, and at all cost.

"Yeah, nothing of real importance happened," Jihad agreed as he signed the paperwork.

After getting that squared away, Amy and Gary went on to explain to Jihad that the investigation was taking a turn. They were no longer as interested in catching Gustavo Santana. They had decided to step over him and try to go for the big fish, Curtis "Black" Campbell. As it turns out, they had been trying to catch Black for years, but he always outsmarted them. Every time they thought they finally had him, he'd get away on a technicality, a witness would go missing, or paperwork was "misplaced." It was obvious Black had a lot of connects in the courts and on the streets. With Jihad working as head of security for Gus, and Gus working directly with Black, all Jihad had to do was get enough conversations on record with Black discussing his illegal business ventures. Jihad was briefed and overloaded with information, such as names and locations of associates of Black so he'd know what to try to bring up in conversations. He was then given a key to the Marriott Hotel on City Line Avenue. He was instructed to meet with Vickie who was expecting him. Jihad exited from the van, then went into Pathmark to buy a soda in order to not look so suspicious going from the van right into another car.

A few minutes after leaving Pathmark, he was on the third floor of the Marriott swiping the card at the door that read 307. On the other side of the door, he walked in on yet another surprise. The room was filled with the strong aroma of weed. As Vickie was explaining to Jihad that the weed smoke was used to further the realization of her character as the thug-loving, ride-or-die hood bitch, he paid little attention. He was more interested in the short Daisy Dukes that hugged tightly around Vickie's fat round ass. She wore a pair of white go-go boots that came just past her calves and rocked a tight wife beater that exposed her perfectly melon-round titties. She even had a teardrop tattoo on the side of her right eye. Jihad was wondering if part of bringing realization to their character was going to allow them to really fuck.

Twenty minutes later, Jihad called Gus as he was instructed to. Gus notified him that they had just left the mall and were within fifteen minutes of Philly. They agreed to meet back up at the hotel. Before disconnecting, he let Jihad know that he would call once they were outside. When Jihad hung up the phone, Vickie leaned over his neck and sucked until a huge passion mark was visible. Jihad took it as Vickie making advances toward him, but she quickly checked him after he took a grab at her ass.

"Listen, Jihad, you have to control yourself. This is nothing more than business. It will never be more than that. Do you understand? Because if you make another move like the one you just made without a good reason, it's going to be a problem," she snapped before she finished blowing the fake weed on her clothes and hair. She smelled like she'd been smoking all day. Next, she pulled an eye drop bottle out and placed several drops of the liquid into her eyes, which made them bloodshot red.

As they waited patiently for Gus, Vickie reminded Jihad to remain calm and normal, as if she was any other hood bitch, and to always follow her lead.

When Gus arrived, he called Jihad to tell him that he was outside. He and Vickie left the room and headed out of the hotel lobby. Once outside, they spotted Black's 850 parked next to the Charger. Vickie wasted no time getting right into character, as she put on the walk that a bitch puts on after getting the shit fucked out of her. She slowly swished her fat ass from side to side in a way that any looker would say, *Damn, she walking like that thing hurt.* Black and Gus sat in the 850 staring in disbelief, wondering how Jihad must be feeling at that very minute, knowing that he just had his way with the little thick stallion. They both silently fantasized how they would have fucked her if they were Jihad. Jihad knew that the men were envious, so he winked his eye and flashed a smile. Gus exchanged a few words with Black before departing and hopping into the Charger. Before Black pulled off, he gave Jihad an approving head nod which Jihad returned with a fight-the-power fist. He and Vickie then got into the backseat of the car.

"Gus, this my little Spanish mommy, Vickie. Baby, this my man, Gus."

"Nice meeting you. You know how to get down Cambridge?"

"Goddamn, Ma, first things first . . . That weed smell too strong. If we get pulled over, they gonna want to search the car. I can't stand that right now, you dig me?" said Gus while staring at Vickie through the rearview mirror, noticing that her eyes were cherry red.

"I got you, Papi. I got some smell goods in my purse. This nigga just wore a bitch out, and I had to smoke," said Vickie as she applied body fragrance on her clothes and hands. They pulled off en route to North Philly.

Fifteen minutes later, they were pulling up on Seventh and Cambridge. Vickie instructed him which house to pull up in front of. She thanked him for the ride before requesting Jihad walk her to the door. Standing in the doorway, Vickie placed her arms around Jihad and began kissing him passionately. As they locked lips, he reached behind her and grabbed a handful of her fat ass. The entire act was deliberately carried out in front of Gus to make sure he never doubted that she really fucked with Jihad. Gus snickered and silently gave mad props to his boy for bagging a cute bitch like her. It was undeniable Vickie was a bad bitch, and if Gus was single, he would've probably told Jihad to let him hit it. He turned away and let the two lovebirds do them.

While observing his surroundings, he spotted several Spanish men and a few blacks operating a drug enterprise right there before his eyes. Their system seemed unique. The customers would pay one of the men, who, in turn, would enter a house and notify one of his partners of the orders. The partner would then go outside and serve them. The flow of customers on the block was rapid and consistent. They were on and off the block like an express line at a shopping center. When Jihad got back into the car, Gus inquired about the block.

"You know who run this joint? It look like a gold mine out here."

"Nah, I don't know, but my bitch probably do. These her peoples down here. You want me to see what it's hitting for?"

"Yeah, most definitely. I was taught to never limit my hustle. Plus, I got that work in for real," Gus boasted.

"Yeah, I'ma get right at her. Anyway, how things go at the mall? I know you picked out something exclusive."

"Damn, I almost forgot. Look at this pretty mafucka here. I got a good deal on it too," said Gus while passing him the gift bag that held the ring in a leather-bound jewelry box. Once Jihad opened the box up, he was stunned by the beauty of the huge, colorful diamond ring. He let out a loud, long whistle as he examined the ring.

"Son, you outdid yourself. Trish is going to love it." Jihad approved.

The Warning

Sha'Ron's phone had been ringing off the hook all afternoon. He refused to take the call because the caller blocked their number. However, he eventually got impatient with the caller and answered.

"Who the fuck is this calling my phone from a private number?" he barked into the receiver.

"Pipe the fuck down, little nigga. This Leaf . . . I don't want nobody to have my new digits for now; that's why I blocked my number. But, anyway, where you at? I need to holla at you ASAP."

"Leaf, you got a lot of explaining to do. You don't reach out to nobody for days, not even to let us know what's good with you, and then you just call me out of the blue like everything all good. You got it fucked up, bro," said Sha'Ron setting the record straight.

"Who the fuck you think you talking to like that? You been hanging around that faggot-ass nigga Gus too long. You niggas is just hustlers. Did you forget *I'm* the killer, little nigga? Come out your mouth like that again, you might find yourself on the other side of the barrel. Now, I was calling you to offer you a position with my new family, but obviously, you ain't ready for that. You rather live in Gus's shadow. But, here's what you can do . . . Give that mafucka a message. Let him know that I'm ready take over this city. Now, if he's smart, he's gonna talk to Mom and Aunt Connie and get them on board so everybody knows to stay the fuck outta my way. My goons trained to kill so—"

Sha'Ron cut him off.

"Nigga, you done lost your mind! You should have known not to offer me no shit like that because you know I would never go against my family. Born a Santana and I'ma die a Santana. So you telling me you so high in the clouds that you're willing to go against your own flesh and blood? So you trying to tell me you willing to shoot our own mother for your fucking pride? Fuck you and fuck your threats. They ain't stop making guns after making yours," voiced Sha'Ron before hanging up. He had allowed his brother to take him off his square and stoop down to his level. He hated letting his emotions get the best of him. No doubt, he loved his brother to death, but he was completely against his actions.

He drove through the city, attempting to clear his mind. While doing so, a weird aura filled the car. Deep down inside, he felt as if this whole situation was about to be blown out of proportion. Now he understood what his mom and aunt were talking about when they said they had a bad feeling. He only hoped none of his loved ones would be seriously hurt from it.

Happy Days

Later on that night when Gus and Jihad returned home, Trish and Connie harassed him continuously about the ring. Gus repeatedly insisted that it was a surprise and wasn't to be shown until the day of the wedding. They had no choice but to respect his wishes.

The following day a wedding planner came over. While they were in the living room discussing preparations, Connie and Trish were back at their old tricks. They stationed themselves directly outside the living room to eavesdrop. When Gus became aware of this, he put them on blast.

"Mom! Trish! Come out here right now!" When they complied, he continued.

"This man is charging me by the hour. This is my surprise to my soon-to-be wife. Now, y'all done got on my last nerve. Take this money and go shopping. Y'all gots to go," he demanded while passing them all the money he had in his pockets and pushing them toward the door. They found the whole thing funny.

Once he got them out of the house, he continued on with his wedding planner. After going over several package deals, he selected the one that best suited the occasion. It consisted of a master chef that would be responsible for designing a custom menu consisting of lamb, filet mignon, and fish. There was to be vegetable, fruit, and potato salads to complement the feast. The cake would have five tiers, each having its own flavor of caramel, fudge, vanilla, strawberry, and cheesecake cream filling. The cake was going to have a diamond pillow-top exterior and was set to stand at four feet tall. He decided the only alcohol he would permit was wine and champagne because he knew how niggas reacted with beer and liquor, and he didn't want to risk any disturbance at the function.

He had chosen a Winter Wonderland black-tie affair and he was excited to see everything come to fruition. He couldn't wait to see the look on Trish's face when she walked in to the reception hall. Once everything was situated with the planner, he called Black to inform him of the progress. Black had a surprise in store for him as well.

"Listen here, youngin', your ol' head done came through for you. Remember my people who let us use the jet to take that trip awhile back?"

"Yeah, I remember. The one you said plays professional sports, right?"

"Yeah, that's the one. Well, check it out . . . He got a mansion over in Gladwyne with a backyard the size of a football field. He's going to let us hold it down for the wedding . . . and that's just half of it. As a token of my appreciation, I've personally made arrangements for you and your wife to be flown to the Cayman Islands for y'all honeymoon. You the young prince, so it's only right that you enjoy the fruits of your labor. What do you think?"

"Damn, ol' head, you like the father I never had. Me making moves with you is the best thing that ever happened for me. I love you, man."

"The feeling mutual, youngin'. I'ma get you later," replied Black.

The final surprise for the wedding came later that night, when his mother pulled him aside to pass him a card that read, *Mom Dukes got connections too.* "This is the number to the lead singer of Jagged Edge. He's in the city on standby, waiting on your phone call. Be creative."

After taking his mother's advice under consideration, he spent the entire night brainstorming. The next morning during breakfast, he put his plan into action.

"Damn, Trish, I know you ain't no morning person, but what's up with your hair? You need to go down and get that taken care of ASAP. The wedding is a few days away, and then you could just get it touched up."

"It look that bad? Connie, you feel like going down Harlem's with me?"

"I don't care. I'll take you as soon as I get out of the shower," Connie responded.

During the time it took them to get themselves together and get down there, Gus had already organized his surprise. As Trish had her head under the dryer, she closed her eyes relaxing while the warm air soothed her scalp. When the dryer cut off, so did her relaxation. When she came up to see what the problem was, she was blown away by who she came face-to-face with. The lead singer of Jagged Edge was on one knee holding a box open, displaying the ring. He then started singing his smash hit, "Let's Get Married."

"Meet me at the altar in your white dress, we ain't getting no younger, we might as well do it! Let's get married."

Trish melted as tears of joy filled her eyes and her hands shook uncontrollably. After he placed the ring on her finger, he gave her a message from Gus.

"Your soon-to-be husband wants to let you know that he's the luckiest man in the world to have a woman like you by his side. He loves you more than life itself. He yearns for the day, the hour, the minute, and the second that you become his wife." Gus completed the scene when he walked in and placed a warm kiss on her forehead. Everybody inside the hair salon gave their congratulations and approval with applause. They had never been catered to or showered with gifts at this rate.

Snake in the Grass

When Leaf got wind of the wedding, he decided that the day it was supposed to take place would be the day when the takeover took effect. Everybody who the Santanas supplied, he planned to shut down their arrangements and enforce his own. His goons were on standby, anticipating that moment.

The day of the wedding finally came. The weather was sunny and beautiful. Everything went as planned. Trish wore a stunning white Vera Wang mermaid dress that hugged her curves as it was designed exclusively for her body. She wore a diamond princess crown similar to the ones the twins wore at their party. Along with it was a cathedral veil that cascaded down her backside. The perfect touch was a rhinestone-beaded appliqué belt that tied everything together. She looked amazing.

Gus sported an all-white tux that was hand stitched by Giorgio Armani's tailor. His wrist was complemented by an antique Rolex Yacht-Master. All the Santanas were present, with the exception of Leaf, for the beautiful ceremony. The lead singer of Jagged Edge performed several hits off his new album. Everything turned out exactly as Gus had wanted it. Trish was taken aback when she walked in to the reception. She felt as if she had stepped into a different dimension and was navigating through a real winter wonderland. Gus could not have asked for more. His wedding was like nothing anyone had ever seen.

Toward the end of the festivities, Gus and Trish rode off in an antique all-white Rolls-Royce provided by his best man and boss, Black. They were now husband and wife, en route to the airport where the jet was awaiting their arrival. Their wedding had set the example to all major hustlers that attended or heard about it—how a true boss was supposed to carry out his wedding.

The Takeover in Effect

"Many men . . . Many, many, many, many men wish death upon me . . . blood in my eyes, dawg, and I can't see. I'm tryin' to be what I'm destined to be, and niggas tryin' to take my life away. I put a hole in nigga for fuckin' with me, my back on the wall, now you gon' see. Better watch how you talk when you talk about me 'cause I'll come and take your life away."

50 Cent rapped as his violent lyrics cranked through the stereo system. This was the music Leaf decided to ride out to. It was gangsta music at its best, putting him in the mood needed for the task ahead. As he drove to his first destination, he played it on full blast. Leaf was followed by a fleet of tinted-out Crown Victorias filled to capacity with goons.

When they pulled up on Fifty-fourth Street, over a dozen hustlers were gathered outside the Chinese store. The nigga that ran the block sat close by inside the Lexus, counting up money. Leaf, EZ, and Ikeal stepped out of the truck and approached the corner. When Crock spotted them, he stepped out of his car and walked over to them.

"Leaf, what's popping, homie? These niggas with you?" he questioned suspiciously while staring the strangers down. At that moment, the back windows to the Crown Victorias slowly rolled down, and barrels of assault rifles were aimed at the corner.

"Yeah, all of these niggas with me. In fact, this my new family. However, I ain't come out here for all that."

"Well, what the fuck you come out here for? I ain't call y'all. And what the fuck is the guns for?"

Crack! Ikeal smacked him upside his head with his Mac-10. He lost his balance and fell to the ground. His temple was ruptured and blood flowed freely. His workers didn't dare react while those rifles were trained on them.

Now that they had everybody's undivided attention, Leaf continued where he left off.

"Now, you pussies listen up. Whoever used to supply this corner, we shutting them down. If it ain't our product being moved out here, then we shutting this mafucka down too. In that case, we will put our own workers out here. So, it's a lose-lose situation for you niggas. Try some slick shit and we will air this bitch out every chance we get. Now, get your bitch ass up before we leave you down there permanently," he threatened. When Crock got to his feet, EZ walked over to the truck and removed a City Blue bag containing four bricks of coke. He then walked up to Crock and pushed the book bag into his chest.

"I know you used to pay nineteen a pop, but I got goons to feed, so the price jumps to twenty-two apiece. I'll be expecting a call from you in the next few days. Everything go as it supposed to, we could avoid shit like this from happening," Leaf voiced before getting back into the truck and proceeding on to the next block. Not only was Crock disrespected in front of his workers, but he felt raped of his heart, pride, and block.

Leaf and his goons repeated the same approach and methods through dozens of other territories and corners supplied by the Santanas. When it was all said and done, they had murdered one hustler who refused to go against the Santanas and put over forty bricks on the street.

They instilled fear in the hearts of many. It wasn't long before the streets were talking. The word was out that Leaf and his South Philly peoples had shut the Santanas down and anybody who opposed would find themselves in a fucked-up situation. Niggas knew that Leaf was a problem by himself, but with the South Philly niggas backing him, he was a dangerous movement.

Testing Patience

Word traveled fast, and when Black caught wind of it, he vowed to have Leaf and his "toy soldiers" disposed of. There was no way he would allow his empire to crumble on behalf of a loose cannon, even if he was a Santana. Black didn't like Leaf from the very beginning, and he had never agreed to fuck with him in the first place. He knew Gus was the backbone of the Santanas' organization, and the twins were the head. He was well aware that going after Leaf might put an end to his long-standing relationship with the Santanas, so he had to put a lot of thought into how he was going to handle everything.

The way Leaf had gone about shit basically told Black the little nigga was challenging him as well. Compared to the niggas Black had on line, Leaf and his "toy soldiers" were PG-13. His niggas were rated R. They would easily be outnumbered, outgunned, and murdered. All it took was for Black to pick up the phone and dial a number. After closely thinking the matter through, he decided to handle this one situation differently from his usual protocol. This pass was on the strength of the Santanas' history with him. If not for that, Leaf would have met a very horrific demise. Instead of placing the call to his henchmen, he placed the call to Jihad. The call was brief and right to the point.

"Listen here. You know who this is, right?"

"Yeah, I know who this is, ol' head. What it do?"

"I'ma meet you outside Gus's spot in about thirty minutes. This is an urgent matter, so be ready and don't be late, understood?"

"Yeah, I understand, ol' head. I'm actually there now, so I'll see you when you get here," stated Jihad before disconnecting the call.

"Come on, Connie, you got to get up. This nigga, Black, going to be here in a half hour. He said he got to holler at me about something urgent. Stop, girl, I ain't playing with you. Come on, Connie . . . Damn, girl. You going to make me do something to you," he moaned as Connie provided him with oral pleasure that was good enough to make his toes curl up. The more he told her to stop, the more she persisted. When he reached his full length, that was the point of no return. He did just what she wanted him to. Once he escaped the tight grips of her powerful jaws, he flipped her over in doggie-style position and thrust himself inside her. He started off with long, deep strokes that caused her juices to flow irregularly. He smacked her ass, encouraging her to fuck him back. She began throwing her ass back with as much force as he applied, while talking dirty to him.

"Come on, Jihad, baby. Fuck me harder! Take that pussy, baby! Hurt me! I love the way you make this pussy feel. Oh, daddy! Daddy! I'm about to come! Oh . . . Come with me, baby . . . Come in my pussy! I'm coming!" Good sex and dirty talk were the perfect combination needed for satisfying relief, which the couple achieved together. Afterward, they lay on the bed out of breath, still climaxing from the aftershock. When Jihad's cell phone went off, he remembered the scheduled meeting with Black. He jumped out of bed and answered the phone, while struggling to get dressed at the same time.

"My fault, ol' head. I'm coming out right now."

"Man, didn't I tell you this was urgent? I don't got time to be playing no games. Hurry up."

The first thing Jihad noticed upon sitting in the passenger seat was the murderous expression written over Black's face. Black stared him up and down several times before he spoke.

"What's going on with you? Did I disturb something? Where Connie at? She in there?" he asked suspiciously.

"Huh? I'm . . . I'm good. I don't know if Connie in there or not. I was downstairs working out. But, what's up? You said something urgent came up, right?" he inquired, quickly changing the conversation.

"I don't know what you know about me, but if you heard I had a bad temper and a short fuse, it was indeed an understatement. I assume that since Gus is on vacation, no one has a clue about the stunts this character, Leaf, has been carrying out. This peon has been running around with a bunch of gun-toting amateurs saying he's taking shit over. He keeps this shit up and he's going to possibly fuck up a good thing that your man Gus worked hard to achieve. When shit gets fucked up for your man, it gets fucked up for me. The usual penalty is a million deaths for a coward, but this one has blood ties to people I have love for. I don't like to see my loved ones suffer from grief, so what I'ma do is put it in y'all hands. Hopefully, y'all can fix this problem before it becomes a headache. I ain't took a Tylenol since I been in this business. Do you get my point?"

"Definitely. I'ma talk to Connie as soon as I get back inside."

"I thought you said you ain't know where she was at."

"She . . . She probably in there upstairs." Jihad tried to quickly cover his tracks.

"Well, fuck all that. It ain't my business. Just make sure y'all fix that problem," he demanded in a voice so chilling that it caused Jihad to briefly shiver, as if a cold winter breeze had hit him.

When Blood Gets Thinner Than Water

Once he went back inside the house, he informed Connie of the situation at hand. Her entire face turned red, and she bit down on her lip so hard that she drew blood. Stomping over to the closet, she retrieved a weapon from a shoe box. After she slipped into a sweat suit, she instructed Jihad to take a ride.

A half hour later, they were pulling up in Sygon Projects down in South Philly. The Range Rover stood out like a sore thumb among the junked-up cars that were parked in front of the projects.

"Pull up right there!" yelled Connie, referring to the benches where a group of young niggas were posted up. She jumped out of the Range with her face twisted up, calling shots.

"Where the fuck is Leaf at?" When no one answered, she snapped.

"Oh, you little mafuckas don't hear me?"

Click! Clack! She cocked the .40 cal back, then continued interrogating the young niggas.

"Y'all hear me now? Y'all go tell the little pussy to come out here. Connie Santana needs to have a word with him immediately. If he ain't out here in five minutes, I'ma air this mafucka out," she threatened before turning her back on them and getting back inside the Range. She overheard one of them explaining on their cell phone what was going on and asking how to take care of it. The other caller must have told them to stand down because he frowned with disappointment and stayed seated.

A few minutes later, she noticed a group of men walking in her direction with three feisty pit bulls that were growling and barking with aggression. One of the men walking over was Leaf. Not wanting to give off the impression that she was intimidated in the tiniest way, she stepped out of the truck with her gun visibly hanging out of her pocket. Leaf approached her in a disrespectful manner, allowing the pit bull whose leash he held to jump at her as if it wanted to attack her. The words he chose to address her with were even more vulgar than his demeanor.

"What the fuck you think you doing, Connie? You coming down here being real disrespectful. You lucky you ain't get yourself shot or killed. These ain't your puppets. What the fuck you supposed to do? Stop my movement? You a bitch, and I'm a man. You ain't on my level. Now, get the fuck out of here and don't ever come back through here," he shouted, causing the dogs to get more aggressive. Connie's anger got the best of her. She pulled the .40 out and shot Leaf's dog four times in the head. With the speed of light, she got the drop on Leaf. With her gun pressed under his chin, she reminded him how she earned the reputation for being a vicious bitch.

"If you wasn't my sister's son, I'd blow your fucking head off! Ain't on your level? Nigga, I do circles around you walking backward," she boasted. Her eyes were bloodshot red and her face was expressionless, like a true killer's. Ikeal and EZ stood close by. They were instructed that this was family business and no matter what, they were not to get involved.

"Don't you ever in your fuckin' life think you can speak to me like that again," Connie said as she spat straight into Leaf's face. If Jihad hadn't jumped out and intervened, she would have probably pistol-whipped him. Even while Jihad pulled her to the car, she never lowered her gun. She kept it aimed at his face while making promises.

"You must have lost your goddamn motherfucking mind pulling this shit. And you're a fucking coward for doing it while Gus is away. That's some real snake shit right there. Stay the fuck away from my family's ventures! If I got to come back down this bitch, *you dead!* I swear on my life. You disowned as a Santana, motherfucker. If you ever come at me like that again, you gonna end just like this dog." She kicked the dead dog and walked back to her car.

As they were pulling off, the Range was hit with a barrage of bullets. They had to duck down low to avoid getting hit. Jihad had to drive and hold Connie down at the same time. She desperately wanted to return fire. However, they were outgunned, and to pop your head up during the attack was suicidal.

"Fall back," Leaf yelled at his men. "Where the fuck do you get off shooting without my saying so? Fuck is wrong with all of you?" Leaf went off at the men that had just shot up his aunt's car. As much as he popped off at the mouth and was trying to take over, truth was, he would never want to physically hurt his family. All Leaf ever really wanted was to get the respect he felt he deserved from his family. He was tired of being in his big cousin's shadow, and he felt this was the only way for him to prove to everybody that he could be a leader just like Gus.

"Don't y'all ever in your fucking life shoot at my aunt or my mother. You understand me?" he yelled out loud enough for everyone to hear. He knew his aunt was going to lose her mind even more having gotten shot at. There was no way for her to know the order hadn't come from him. His heart dropped at the thought of what his mother was going to think when his aunt Connie told her what had just gone down.

Mo' Money . . . Mo' Problems

While Gus and Trish were swimming in a remote channel of water playing with live dolphins and enjoying fun in the sun, one of the resort workers came up holding a cordless phone and whispered an important message to him.

"Sir, you have an urgent telephone call from a Mrs. Santana. Would you like to take the call?"

"Yeah, I'll take the call. Just let me step out of here and dry off," he replied before climbing out of the pool. Upon stepping out, he was met by another resort worker holding a robe and towel. Once he gathered himself, he retrieved the phone.

"I hope this is some type of emergency because if I remember correctly, I left specific instructions to not be disturbed during my honeymoon."

"This is your mother, Gus. Leaf just tried to kill me! That slimy nigga shot my truck up along with a bunch of them dirty-ass South Philly niggas. He declared war against us. I need you home *now*," she said. Gus remained silent for a few odd moments before he spoke. He searched for the right words that would comfort his mother. His cousin had crossed the final line, and his actions were inexcusable.

"Mom, calm down. I'm on the first thing out of here. Let me handle this. I don't need you going back to jail. Sit tight. I'll be there as soon as I can," he assured her before hanging up.

Trish watched him the entire time he was on the phone. She could tell by his body language that the call was a disturbing one. If looks could kill, everyone in the resort would be dead. She knew it was time to go, so to speed things up, she emerged from the pool and saved him the trouble of having to inform her that the vacation was over. When he realized she was standing by his side waiting to follow his lead, he gave her a look that told her he appreciated her support and understanding. An hour later, they were on a first-class flight to JFK airport in New York City.

Over the last few weeks, the federal probe into the Black and Santana investigation had progressed significantly. The lead detectives and their associates were very happy with the way things were going. They had labeled the operation, "The Black Spider," because the more they learned about Black, the more they realized he had connections that connected like a spider's web. Their informant and his listening devices were key factors in obtaining all of the intelligence they'd been able to gather so far. Other branches of the FBI had now joined the investigation. Black had so much stuff going on with him, even the IRS had started conducting an investigation, pulling out tax returns dating back a few years. Everyone was highly interested in Curtis "Black" Campbell.

He was no stranger to their task force or the federal court system. A few years back, he was indicted on charges of kidnapping, extortion, and robbery. Their case against him fell apart when the star witness caught a case of amnesia while on the witness stand. He recanted and contradicted his entire statement, so the prosecution had no choice but to withdraw all charges. Now that they had reestablished a more promising chance of indicting him on serious offenses, and they'd be able to use his own recorded conversations to prove his illegal activity, they worked patiently in continuing to build their cases. Today, they went in front of their superiors with a progress report, informing them of the status of the investigation. Once the information was conveyed, the superiors came to their conclusion.

"At this time, we believe that the investigation is moving along in the right direction; however, it is still in the preliminary stages. We need to dig deeper into Mr. Campbell's lead role in the organization. When we present this case to a grand jury, we want to eliminate any shadow of doubt. We want the case loophole proof. Fancy-lawyer proof. The federal system will not be mocked by this individual again. Let's continue the hard work, people. Our resources are limited, so let's use what we've got to get what we want." He concluded the meeting and scheduled the next one for the following month.

When Gus and Trish arrived back in Philadelphia, they were picked up by Jihad and Connie in his BMW. Connie was anxious to speak her piece. She wasted no time expressing how she felt about the situation and how she wanted to handle it.

"The nigga has disgraced our family's name. He tried to kill me. His blood is no longer sacred. I'm not asking you to kill him, I'm *telling* you to. It's the only way I will feel relief again. I don't give a fuck about what anybody has to say. I'm finished with the talking."

"Mom, you got every right to feel the way you do, but I don't think you realize what you're asking me to do." Gus tried to reason with his mother. "You're basically asking me to kill your own sister's son. Your nephew that you've loved as if he was your own son, Ma."

"I know exactly what the fuck I'm asking you to do, Gus. Believe me, I'm hurting deep down inside, but that nigga has lost his mind. I saw him, Gus, and I'm telling you that is *not* my nephew!"

"And how do you think your sister is going to take you asking me to kill her firstborn?"

"I'll cross that bridge when I get there," Connie responded, still not fully thinking about how deep an act like that would cut her sister.

"Okay, Ma, I see I can't talk you out of this right now, so what I'm going to do is give you a few days to cool off, and then I'm only going to ask you one more time if you are sure of your decision. If, after a few days, you still feel the same way, then I've got no choice but to carry out your wishes. Jihad, let's drop the ladies off, and then take a ride," he spoke softly.

While waiting for the darkness of night to provide the cover they needed, they decided to stop at Freeze's to get a platter and a few drinks. Gus hoped not to run into Sha'Ron while down there because he didn't feel ready to explain the situation to him. He was still in disbelief of everything that he'd been told and was having a hard time processing everything. He never expected Leaf to turn on them like that. He had no idea how he was going to break all of this down to Sha'Ron, and especially his aunt Consuela. As they were sitting down at their regular table throwing back shots of Patrón, the nigga, Crock, from Fifty-fourth Street approached the table. Without excusing himself or being acknowledged, he rudely invaded their zone.

"Damn, Gus! What's really good? Your peoples came through my block the other day and got real disrespectful. I ain't no sucker, but I know that's your blood. What am I supposed to do?" This statement prompted Jihad to jump up and position himself for combat.

"Nigga, is you crazy? Don't you know you can get yourself killed, walking up on niggas like that? Back the fuck up and approach this table like you got some respect, nigga," he demanded while giving Crock the stare of death. With a heart full of fear, Crock did just as he was told.

"My fault, Gus. I ain't mean no disrespect. Like I was saying, Leaf and some other niggas came down my block with a bunch of guns. My peoples was ready to go to war, but I couldn't give the word because I know that's your family. The nigga passed me some of his own product, charged me more for it, and told me to call him when I was done. I been finished, but my pride won't allow me to call the nigga. I rather just go through you. I hope after this, shit will be back the way it used to be."

"Where the money at? You got it close by?" Gus inquired.

"I got it outside in my trunk right now," he confirmed. In a matter of a few seconds, Gus had constructed a wicked plot.

"Give me the number he gave you to call."

"215-555-0921."

"All right, that's good. Jihad, follow him outside to his car and get that paper." When Jihad came back in, he carried the money inside a book bag.

"I ain't count it up, but the nigga said it was over eighty thousand. What you up to, nigga? I see that look in your eye."

"You know how it's that one thing that you always promised yourself you would do one day? I'm about to make that shit rain," he snapped before pulling stacks of money from the book bag and carelessly throwing it around the bar. The bar patrons went into a frenzy. They pushed, punched, kicked, and did everything in their power to pick up as much money as they could. The funny thing was, it was a bunch of niggas crawling on the ground for money that claimed to be big-time ballers.

Gus and Jihad walked out the door laughing about the situation. The laughter was soon replaced with murderous intentions as they slowly drove through Sygon Projects. When Gus spotted a few niggas outside trapping, he instructed Jihad to circle the block and park up.

"Keep the shit running and your eyes open," he barked before putting his hood over his head and hopping out of the car.

Jihad became paranoid as hell as he called on his employers to come to his rescue.

"Shit! Amy, if you hear me, we are down South Philly at Sygon Projects. Gus is ready to do something crazy. I'm stuck! What the fuck am I—?"

Suddenly, gunshots rang out in the near distance.

Bomp! Bomp! Bomp! Bomp! Bomp! Bomp! Bomp! Bomp!

"Aw, shit. The nigga done shot at something or someone. Shots fired!" he panicked. Suddenly, the door flew open and Gus hopped in the car out of breath.

"Let's get the fuck out of here. I laid all them niggas out! What the fuck was you in here screaming about?" Jihad ignored the question and focused on getting far away from the area. Once they made it a safe distance away from the scene, Gus put the icing on the cake. He used the number Crock had given him to call Leaf. He got an answer on the first ring.

"Leaf, you a fuckin' coward, nigga. You pull that stunt on my mom while I'm on vacation? You're lucky she let you live, my nigga. By the way, that eighty thousand and change that Crock owed you . . . Well, I made it rain with that shit down at Freeze's. Check for yourself. Your career is finished here, nigga. If I was you, I'd leave the city right now, or else it's going to be an instant repeat of tonight every fuckin' day. I'm back like I never left."

Leaf sat quiet on the other end of the line. Crock had done just as he expected he would do. Before he could respond, the call was disconnected. As he analyzed the situation, he determined that Gus spoke the truth about the money. He had no other way of knowing about it unless it came from Crock. That also explains how he got the number. However, he didn't understand what he meant by doing an instant replay every day. As he sat back pondering on the statement, his thoughts were interrupted by the buzzing of his cell phone. He thought it was Gus calling back with more threats. Once he viewed the caller ID, he noticed that it was Ikeal's number.

"Yo, killer. What the situation?"

"I'm trying to figure something out. Do your peoples got a white BMW?"

"Yeah, why? What's up?" asked Leaf, fearing the worst.

"Them niggas slid through and aired shit out. Two of the young niggas got killed and the other one fighting for his life. This shit can't go unanswered. We ready to move out. What's up?"

"Don't move without me. I'm on my way down there right now!"

Leaf and his goons rode around for an hour searching for Gus, to no avail. The nigga was somewhere in the cut. The only reason they didn't take it to his front door was because there was a possibility that Leaf's mother was in the house. He refused to put his mother in harm's way. They decided to slide past Fifty-fourth Street and pay Crock a visit instead.

Parking a block or so away, they were able to maintain a clear visual of Fifty-fourth Street. The strip was vacant, with the exception of one hustler who used the Chinese store as his station to hustle out of. Just as they were ready to pull off and end the mission until the following day, they spotted Crock's black Lexus pull up in front of the store. He wasn't alone. There was a female companion in the passenger seat. After a few minutes, he jumped out and entered the store. Leaf pulled the truck from the parking space and gunned it to the front of the Chinese store. He put the car in Park and hopped out. When he entered the store, he encountered Crock and his man smoking a Dutch while counting a stack of money. He looked as if he had seen a ghost. He tried to talk himself out of the situation.

"Leaf, what's good? That work was proper. I was just getting ready to hit your phone. Did you get your money from Gus?" he asked with a slight panic in his voice.

Two gunshots sounded off outside. Crock's homie made the fatal mistake of reaching into his coat. Leaf was faster on the draw and splattered his brains on the wall. Crock dropped his head. He was unable to face his soon-to-be killer. Leaf sat him down permanently with two shots to the face. Noticing the Dutch still burning next to the man's body, he walked over, picked it up, and took a deep pull. As he was on his way out of the store, he was stopped in his tracks by the screaming of the Chinese lady who stood behind the bulletproof counter.

"I call police! You crazy! This my store, nigger!"

He pointed his gun in her direction and fired the remaining shots. Although none of the bullets penetrated through, it scared the shit out of her.

When he left the store, he walked to the truck as if he didn't have a care in the world. While passing the Lexus, he glimpsed the female whose body was slumped over the seat suffering from a head shot. Back inside the truck, he offered his goons the Dutch he had taken from the deceased. They shared it as they drove back to South Philly, laughing about their latest kills.

The following morning everyone present in Gus's house was tuned in to the local news. They briefly talked about the shooting down in South Philly that left two people dead and another seriously injured. Shootings in that neighborhood were common on a day-to-day basis and received little or no attention. This was good on their behalf. But when they flashed the breaking news story across the screen, they talked about a triple murder in West Philly on Fifty-fourth Street. They showed pictures of three victims, as well as the gruesome aftermath the killers left behind. Connie stood up and turned the television off.

"That's that nigga's work, ain't it? He's trying to outdo you. That mafucka got the last laugh. He thinks he's winning, Gus. You got to hit him harder, baby," she encouraged.

His mother's crazy, irrational attitude was starting to bother him. Shit was already out of hand. At the rate things were going, his promises of fortune and success were being replaced with death and unnecessary beef with his own blood.

Although Trish didn't say anything, he could see the sadness and fear written all over her face. She looked as if she thought she was going to lose him. Becoming frustrated with the situation, he turned to the only person he knew could think through situations like this and manage to come out on top. Picking up his cell phone, he connected the call.

"Black, what's up with you? Look, I'm back home, and something real urgent has come up. I need to get at you. Can I get up with you?"

"I'm a little tied up with something right now, but you could swing through my house around two thirty. Cool?"

"That's great. That gives me enough time to grab me a rental. I appreciate you, ol' head," he expressed before disconnecting. "Jihad, we gotta roll. We need to pick up another rental, and then we're going to Black's house."

"Trish, Ma, I'll see you ladies later. Ma, calm yourself down, and, Trish, please don't worry, baby," he said to the two most important women in his life. He hated seeing them upset.

While they were on the way to the rental agency, Jihad received an unexpected call from Vickie. He was skeptical about answering it because Gus was in the car with them. On second thought, he decided it might be urgent, so he answered anyway.

"What's up, Ma-Ma? I ain't hear from you in a minute. What made you hit me up out of the blue?"

"Listen very closely, Jihad. We've been following everything that's been going on, and we're close to making a few arrests. However, there's one last thing we need you to put into place before that happens. I need you to stop by my place before y'all go over to Black's house. We've already created a scheme that's convincing enough for him to bring you through here. I don't feel good. I missed my period, and I think I'm pregnant . . . react shocked," she instructed.

"What? Are you serious?" he replied perfectly.

"Okay, good. Now when you guys switch cars, drive to Rite Aid and pick up a pregnancy test. Once you get here, just follow my lead."

"Damn! You fucked my head up with that one. I'd never thought in a million years, I'd be a father." When he hung the phone up, Gus inquired with curiosity.

"That was the little Spanish mommy? Is she all right?"

"Yeah, she good, but the bitch scaring me, talking that pregnancy shit. I need to grab a test and stop by her spot immediately."

Being a regular at the car rental agency came with advantages, and quick, top-of-the-line service was one of them. He chose the smoked-out Lincoln Continental, and they were back on the road by twelve forty-five. At that time, Jihad explained deeper the dilemma that was happening with Vickie. He requested if they could stop at the store, pick up the test, and then go past her house. Gus agreed and was more supportive than expected.

"If she is pregnant, I want to be the godfather, nigga."

"Most definitely!"

After stopping at the drugstore, they headed down to North Philly to Vickie's house. Upon arrival, she answered the door, appearing distraught. Her eyes were puffy, and she wore a blanket covering her shoulders.

"Come on in, y'all. I look a mess. Jihad, come on upstairs. I been holding my pee for twenty minutes. I want to hurry up and take this test. Gus, make yourself at home, baby," she invited in a welcoming manner as she and Jihad headed upstairs. Once inside the bathroom, Vickie quickly handed him two small devices that looked like miniature speakers. She placed a note in front of him that read, *Plant at least one of these in Black's house or car . . . both, if possible. Be very careful. Things will be wrapping up shortly.* After relaying the message, she removed the pregnancy test and poured a liquid substance over the top of it. The remainder was poured inside the toilet and flushed. After washing her hands, they went back downstairs where they patiently waited for the results. Five minutes later, Jihad did the honors of reading it.

"It's two lines on it. What that mean?"

"That mean I'm pregnant, nigga. I told you to stop coming up in me like that! You know your ass is fertile from being in jail all that time."

"Gus, I can't believe this shit! Am I reading this right?" he questioned while showing him the results.

"Hell, yeah, you reading it right. The two lines is clear as day. You going to be a father, nigga."

"It is what it is, Vickie. I be back later tonight. Take this couple dollars and feed my baby," he stated before peeling off a few hundred-dollar bills. When he started kissing on her stomach and talking like a baby, Gus took his cue to leave.

"Yo, I'ma be out in the car. Don't forget to check on what we talked about last time when we was down here."

"I got you, homie. I be right out." As soon as Gus left, she reminded him one last time of his assignment.

"Remember, Jihad, one of those needs to be placed in Black's house. In the sofa, bathroom, under the table, anyplace where he's likely to converse. He still wants to know about setting up shop on this block? Shit! If he only knew, these niggas ready to get indicted they damn self. We'll be listening very closely. Continue the good job and follow our lead," she encouraged before sending him on his way. When Jihad got back in the car, he made something up to tell Gus.

"I asked about the block, and she said she was going to holler at her peoples, and then get back to me."

Thirty minutes later, they were walking into Black's King of Prussia home. Black wasted no time letting Gus know he knew about everything going on. He even told him that he had called Jihad and spared Leaf's life out of respect for him and his family.

"I appreciate that, ol' head."

"Don't mention it. Now, was y'all able to straighten that problem out with your peoples?"

"That nigga ain't my people no more. For one, he opposed against everything we stand for. Then to make matters worse, he transgressed against my mother. I told the nigga, the best thing for him would be to leave town. Because if not, shit is just gonna keep getting messy. I'ma kill everything around him until he has no choice but to leave. You dig me?"

Black turned his back to Gus. He didn't want to expose the disappointment that was clearly written on his face. He realized that Gus wasn't willing to kill Leaf. He knew they were cousins and everything, but Gus should've been prepared to kill Leaf for the way he'd disrespected his mother and how he came for his empire. He'd warned Jihad in hopes that they would handle the situation, but apparently he was mistaken. This proved to Black that Gus was a weak nigga after all. Placing his hand on his chin, he began contemplating on the appropriate actions he had to take that would eliminate his association to the Santanas.

"Good. Good. That's what I like to hear. Now, we got to focus on getting back to work. Let's go out back and talk real quick. Please excuse us, Jihad." Black had to keep up the act that he was cool with everything that was going on. He led the way for Gus to follow him toward the outside patio.

Gus had no idea that his actions had just cost him his relationship with his mentor. He thought he was making Black proud with the way he was handling everything, but he was sadly mistaken. He was under the impression that Black condoned him sparing his cousin's life. But instead, Black was now ready to turn his back on him and the twins. Black refused to get himself involved or caught up with street wars. They usually ended with one of two outcomes. Everyone would end up dead or in jail. His empire was too valuable to take either risk. They all had to die. All the love that he once had for Gus ceased from existence. It was replaced with a plot and a death wish.

With Gus and Black out of the room, Jihad was presented the perfect opportunity to carry out what he was instructed to do. He quickly retrieved the device from his pants and stuffed it inside the couch.

"Listen, Gus, while you were on vacation I came across a new contact with a better grade of work at a cheaper price. He offered me a hundred joints at a monster deal. I'm supposed to get with him tonight, but I can't go withdraw that kind of money from the bank in that little bit of time. Can you get your hands on about two million?"

"I got a little bit more than that saved up, but I trust you with it. I'll have to take a ride out to Jersey to get it, though. How soon you need it?"

"The sooner the better," he claimed. Black had indeed initiated the first act of rocking a nigga to sleep, and that was by breaking him financially. That characteristic made him a master at being treacherous and deceptive. These elements alone were key factors in him maintaining his reign on the top over the years.

When they returned to the living room, they both took notice of Jihad. Not only was his forehead sweating profusely, but he also appeared to be a nervous wreck. It was obvious he wasn't aware of it.

"Little homie, what's wrong? You seen a ghost?" Black asked suspiciously.

"Huh? What you mean by that? It's hot as shit, and I don't like sitting still," he lied after taking notice of his nervous reaction.

"Anyway, we got to shoot over the bridge real quick so I can grab some paper. Get some air on the way to the car," Gus recommended. Black never took his eyes off of Jihad. He knew he lied about it being hot because his house was always kept cool. *He must have seen the expression on my face when I turned my back on Gus. I wonder if he's on to me*, Black thought as he watched them pull out of the driveway.

"As soon as y'all get back, both of y'all niggas going to get it," he said to himself.

***

During the ride over to New Jersey, the two sat silently, each caught up in deep thought. Something inside Gus was telling him to fall back. His vibes were so overwhelming that it gave him sharp pains in the pit of his stomach. Yet, he ignored the signs and chalked it up to him just being anxious about everything that was going on. Add to that the fact that he'd barely slept since he got back, it definitely could explain why he was feeling some type of way.

Jihad, on the other hand, was scared shitless. He had almost been exposed and feared that when they returned, Black might have discovered the device and kill him on the spot. He had to figure something out—fast. Unbeknownst to him, help was on the way.

Once he successfully planted the bug in Black's house, the warrant to arrest Gus was authorized. They heard over the wire that Gus was planning to retrieve some money over in New Jersey. There was a helicopter hovering in the sky, monitoring their every move and feeding the information to a ground unit that was ready to move out.

When they arrived at the Cherry Hill Manor Apartments, Gus left the car running and informed Jihad that he would be right out. The apartment was fully furnished. Basic yet comfortable. When Gus entered, he walked over to the floor-model television, lifted the panel, and pushed a sequence of different buttons that, in turn, granted him access to the hidden compartment within the foundation. The front of the TV opened up like a door, revealing neatly stacked piles of money. He removed a majority of it before securing the stash spot. Inside the bedroom, he retrieved a large Nike duffle bag which he used to carry the money. Believing that the uncomfortable feeling in his stomach could also be related to him having to relieve his bowels, he went to use the bathroom.

Meanwhile, outside, Jihad was contacted by Amy who informed him of what was ready to take place and further instructed him.

"Jihad, listen very carefully. We're ready to move in on Gus and arrest him. At this time, you need to get behind the wheel of the car and pull off. There will be a Dodge Charger with flashing lights pursuing you. Do not crash, but drive like you are trying to get away. Ditch the car in West Philly and get with Connie. We'll be listening in. Good luck."

Jihad went into action immediately. He was surprised that the Charger hopped on his tail as soon as he turned out of the parking lot. *How the fuck did they get here that fast?* he wondered while pulling off. Through the rearview mirror, he observed four black vans pull up to the apartment and dozens of masked men bearing FBI letters on their vest storming the building. While Gus was sitting on the toilet finishing up his business, his attention was broken by a loud crash coming through the front door. Next, he heard loud voices screaming.

"FBI! FBI! We have a warrant!" as they searched the premises room by room. They discovered Gus in the bathroom, still sitting on the toilet with pants down to his ankles. They didn't have the decency to allow him to wipe his ass. He was snatched up off the toilet and cuffed up. They hauled him outside where they threw him in back of one of the vans. A local news station had arrived and was able to get live footage of Gus before he was placed in the van. Feeling confused and humiliated, Gus demanded an explanation.

"What the fuck is this all about? Y'all ain't catch me with shit. I just stopped here to use the bathroom," he argued.

"I assume you are not going to exercise your right to remain silent. Therefore, I'll inform you that you are being charged with 924C, 848, and 922G, which in federal terms means you are a drug kingpin and a convicted felon, carrying a gun that you used to further your drug trafficking. You are facing thirty years to life. More than likely, you'll be denied bail and housed in the Federal Detention Center until you're brought to trial. I'm sorry to say it, but your only hope of ever making it back on the streets is to cooperate with us," Adam recommended.

"I don't speak rat. My lawyer will challenge all allegations in court. Take me to jail. I ain't got shit to say to y'all," he barked.

"That's okay too. But let me inform you of this, we're nothing like the state. Our conviction rate is 98.9 percent. Fancy lawyers will just take your money and sell you out. They hold no weight. All it takes is word of mouth to get you convicted in front of a jury of upper-class residents. The only thing that matters over here is what you know—nothing else. By the way, whoever your friend was, let him know when you talk to him that when we find the car, we'll have it dusted for prints, and he will be charged with eluding authorities and affecting interstate commerce. He caused a hell of a traffic jam on the Ben Franklin Bridge," Adam added, making sure to throw in a good cover for Jihad.

Gus didn't respond as he soaked in everything the fed said to him. He believed deep down inside that he would get different results than 98.9 percent of the people. He was relieved that Jihad escaped them. He would at least sleep comfortable knowing that he would protect his peoples with his life. As Gus was being transported to the Federal Detention Center, he reflected on the events that led up to him being grabbed by the feds. He wished he would've followed his gut instincts that something wasn't right.

Meanwhile, Jihad had made his way to West Philly. He went through the motions of acting like he had escaped from getting caught by the feds, and he ditched the Lincoln in the back of an auto repair shop just as he'd been told. He had to make sure he did everything just in case someone was watching him. He jogged over a block before contacting Connie.

"What's up, Jihad? What time are y'all coming home?"

"Connie, they got Gus! I can't explain the shit over the phone, though. I need you to come pick me up right now. I'm on Fifty-third and Lancaster Avenue. Hurry up!" he shouted into the phone.

"Jihad . . . Wait a minute! What do you mean? Where is my son at? Where is my motherfuckin' son at?" she snapped.

"The feds rained down on us! I don't know if he locked up or what. I ain't trying to talk over these phones. Come and pick me up."

About ten minutes later, Jihad spotted the BMW pulling into the gas station. He ran across the street and jumped in the back. Connie and Trish hit him with a barrage of questions the second he sat down.

"What the fuck happened? Why he ain't call nobody? What was y'all doing?" They both questioned him with frustration.

"Y'all got to calm down until we find out exactly what's going on. We ain't have shit on us. He just went over to Jersey to get some money. While he was inside, I peeped the feds blitzing the parking lot. I took them mafuckas on a chase the second I see them going into the building that Gus went into. We got to get out of West Philly ASAP before we run into Leaf and them," he relayed with fear and paranoia. "With Gus being locked up, ain't no telling what kind of shit Leaf might try to pull!" Jihad was really on the verge of losing his mind. He didn't know what role he was playing at this point. He couldn't tell if he was acting as an informant or if he was still acting as security.

All of his lies and back-and-forth were catching up, and he was falling apart.

"I wouldn't be surprised if that snake motherfucker is somehow connected to this shit," Connie spat before pulling off.

The Beginning of the Ending

Over in the Federal Detention Center, after being booked, processed, and medically cleared, Gus was placed on 5 north in 507 cell. It was after ten o'clock, so the block was already locked down. The officer working escorted him to the cell and secured him inside. Upon stepping in, he noticed that the majority of the floor was covered in prayer rugs, and there was a younger Muslim man engaging in prayer. Gus stood by the door and waited for him to finish. After completing the prayer, he stood up and introduced himself to the new cellmate.

"Assalamu alaikum. My name is Kalid. Are you Muslim?"

"I used to read up, but I was into too much shit out there to practice. My name's Gus. I had a long day. I'm just trying to climb in the bunk and get some rest."

"Gus, you from West Philly? I heard about you."

"Yeah, that's me. Why? What's up?" he asked in defense.

"No, brother, it ain't like that. I just heard you was out there doing your thing. But anyway, if you need anything, feel free to go in my locker. I keep it stocked up. All I ask is that when you urinate, sit down or take a knee. Go ahead and get you some rest. I'll holla at you in the morning."

Gus made his bed up and climbed in. His night was restless as he tossed and turned, trying to figure out what went wrong and how he landed in the feds. His stress and worries were at an all-time high. The only people that knew he was on his way to New Jersey were Black and

Jihad. He couldn't figure out how the feds knew to find him in that apartment. Shit just wasn't adding up. There had to be a rat somewhere in all of this mess.

Unknown to him, the feds had rats everywhere. They had arranged for him to be housed on that unit, and even that very cell. Kalid was one of the biggest rats in the jail. The feds counted on him to make Gus feel comfortable and open up to him. From there, he could either be persuaded to cooperate or reveal crucial information about his case and other criminal activities. The information would be turned over to the feds, who would surely find a way to put it to use.

Back over at Gus's house, the three sat on the couch tuned into the eleven o'clock news. Before the story aired, they showed Gus's mug shot picture, and then the news camera caught the actual shot of him being tossed into the back of the van.

"This is Shelly Walters, and we're live at the Cherry Hill Manor Apartments. Just hours ago, FBI agents raided an apartment believed to be owned by Gus Santana. When they entered the unit, they discovered a duffle bag filled with close to two million dollars right out in clear view. After doing a sweep of the apartment, we were informed by an inside source that they found the suspect with his pants down, literally. Apparently, he was using the bathroom facilities during the time of the raid. He was arrested without further incident. When authorities noticed the car the suspect arrived in pulling off into traffic, they realized the suspect wasn't alone and gave pursuit. Allegedly, the suspect drove so recklessly during rush-hour traffic that they had no choice but to suspend the chase. Anyone with information leading to the arrest and conviction of this individual is urged to call FBI headquarters at (215) 555-9991. That number again is (215) 555-9991. A source close to the investigation

says that Gustavo Santana is facing a host of serious charges, ranging from drug trafficking to conspiracy and weapons offenses. We're told that more charges are expected to follow. Again, this is Shelly Walters, reporting to you live. Channel Seven, Action News will keep you posted on any new developments."

The news report sent chills through the occupants of the household. They all sat quietly, deep in their own thoughts. The way the news detailed the charges, and possibly more to follow, was overwhelming for the ladies. Connie continued to blame Leaf for her son's situation, while Trish just rocked back and forth, silently processing everything. She had this distant look in her eyes, like she was physically there, but her mind was a million miles away. The scene was too emotional for Jihad to bear. He got up and went to pour himself a drink. He had temporarily forgotten that he was the cause of all this. His heart was racing, and he couldn't make full sense out of things at this point.

They weren't the only ones tuned into the news that night. Sha'Ron and Consuela were viewers as well. Sha'Ron had his own conclusions of why Gus was faced with trials and tribulations.

"Shit happens for a reason, Mom. Maybe it's for the best that Gus got locked up because the way Leaf been popping off, I'm surprised they ain't have a shoot-out yet. I still can't believe the way Leaf came at me like we wasn't brothers. I'm telling you, Ma, he was tripping," Sha'Ron reiterated to his mother for the second time. He had told her about the last conversation he'd had with Leaf and how Leaf seemed determined to start his own thing separate from what they had all built together. Sha'Ron still didn't understand why his brother was so hell-bent on breaking up the family.

"If Gus didn't get locked up, he would have most likely killed Leaf, putting me in a fucked-up position to have to avenge my brother's death. They both my blood, but Leaf is my brother. He a wild nigga and don't use his head half the time, but he still my brother. I bet Connie think that Leaf got something to do with this arrest too."

"Yeah, knowing my sister, she's probably thinking that Leaf snitched so he could get Gus out of the way so he can take over." Consuela put in her two cents.

"I don't know, Mom. All of this is getting out of hand, if you ask me. I'm still pretty mad at Leaf, but I'm gonna be the bigger person in this. I think it's time that I step in between this mess and try to resolve it before Gus come back home and somebody gets hurt or killed for real," Sha'Ron said, standing to his feet.

"You right, baby. I need to go pay Connie a visit and get to the bottom of all this. I'm going to see what I can do to help Gus out and try to ease the tension at the same time. Be careful, baby."

"I'm good, Mom. I'm just trying to move on from this shit and put it behind us. I'ma call one of Leaf's close female friends and see if I can get a message over to him. He still ain't given me his new number."

For the first time in years, Black's hesitation and greed had placed him in a very uncomfortable position. After he watched the news and became aware of Gus's situation, he wished that he would have killed the niggas when they were in his home earlier that day, as he was supposed to. Now, he stressed about whether Gus would rat him out to save his own ass. Sure, Gus had passed the test down in Brazil, but he hadn't been caught carrying a bag with $2 million in it. Black was worried about what

Gus would and wouldn't do. He'd been in their system once and witnessed how they managed to break the best of them. A serious chess match lay before him, but there was one person who he personally blamed for initiating this whole mess. He would be eliminated before the game even started. Picking up his Nextel phone, he chirped one of his most respected henchmen. Seconds later, a deep voice came over the airwaves.

"Yo, how can I be of service?" asked Colt.

"The situation we discussed the other day needs to be attended to ASAP!"

"I'm right on top of it, homie. Say no more," Colt responded excitedly.

Reconcile Differences

Later on that night while Sha'Ron was in the house watching a movie, the call he had placed to Nicki, Leaf's friend, was returned. She informed him that she had talked to Leaf a few minutes ago, and she told Sha'Ron that he was down at Freeze's. Sha'Ron planned on telling his brother that he needs to tell his girls not to give up his whereabouts to just anyone that calls. If he had been an enemy, she would've just given them the perfect setup to get his brother killed. When he called her, he hadn't told her who he was, so it was pretty stupid of her to call him back and give him all of that information without hesitation. That could have been dangerous had it been someone else. Sha'Ron turned off the television, and then headed down to the bar.

When he arrived, he spotted Leaf in the back appearing disoriented. He was seated next to some skeezer who was making facial expressions, as if she was engaged in some sort of sexual encounter. Walking closer to his table, he discovered why she was making those faces, and why his brother appeared the way he did. There was an empty bottle of syrup on the table and several shots of liquor. Leaf's hand was under the skeezer's dress, moving back and forth. When he spotted Sha'Ron, he took his hand from under her dress and placed it under his coat.

"What's up, nigga? You thought I was going to let you creep up on me? I stay strapped," he reminded his little brother while revealing the handle of his gun. His voice was slurred, and his eyes were barely open.

"I ain't come here for all that bullshit, Leaf. C'mon, drop the shit. You're my brother. Listen, shit done got hectic. Gus got gripped up by them alphabet boys, and shit ain't looking good for him."

"And? What the fuck that got to do with me? Fuck that nigga," Leaf responded as he picked up his cup of liquor and took a deep gulp.

"Excuse me, sweetheart. Let me holla at this nigga in privacy real quick," he requested from his female companion. After she got up and excused herself from the table, they continued where they left off.

"Leaf, that shit could affect all of us. At one time, we were all eating off the same table."

Leaf's head suddenly fell down to his chest, and his eyes rolled into the back of his head.

"Leaf, wake up! I got to take you home, nigga." Leaf was so twisted, he nodded off in the middle of the conversation. Sha'Ron tried to shake him awake to no avail. He was comatose. The little skeezer walked back over after noticing what was going on. Sha'Ron figured he'd put her to good use, so he grabbed Leaf's car keys off the table and gave her instructions.

"Listen, sweetheart, I need you to go out front and get Leaf's truck, then pull it up out back. You think you can handle that?" he asked before handing her the keys.

"Of course I can handle that. I'm a rider, boo," she claimed while taking the keys. Sha'Ron, with the assistance of a mutual associate, carried Leaf out back and placed him in the passenger seat of the truck. The skeezer got the wrong impression, thinking she would be trusted to care for his brother in that condition. He quickly dismissed her.

"All right, thank you, but I got it from here. I'ma take him home and make sure he good. I'll let him know you helped out. Matter of fact, take this couple of dollars."

He gave her a few fifties before climbing in and pulling off. Along the way, he called Nicki to inform her of the situation.

"Nicki, it's Sha'Ron." This time making sure she knew who she was talking to. "I need you to come downstairs and open the front door. The nigga Leaf is wasted. You've got to help me bring him inside. I be there in like five minutes."

"All right, Sha'Ron, let me slide something on. That boy get on my nerves with that high shit," she spat before disconnecting the call. Sha'Ron was so busy worrying about his brother, he never took notice of the car following him at a close distance.

A few minutes later, he was pulling up in front of Overbrook Park Apartments. Nicki came out, shortly afterward. Together, they assisted Leaf inside by supporting his arms over their shoulders. It took them five minutes to get him into the apartment. After laying him on the couch, Nicki started to pat his face down with a rag and cold water. Once Leaf responded to the water being placed on his face, Sha'Ron was certain that he was going to be okay. Before leaving, he asked Nicki to give Leaf a message once he snapped out of his high.

"Tell him I love him, and we got to move on from the dumb shit. We all brothers. I got to get back down Freeze's to get my car, and I'ma see if I can get somebody to drive his truck back up here. Keep looking after this crazy nigga. Thanks for holding him down. If you need me, give me a call."

"Thank you, Sha'Ron. His dumb ass lucky he got a brother like you that really loves him."

After Sha'Ron got back into the truck, he searched through his cell phone for someone who he could pick up to follow him back there so he could park his brother's truck up. Suddenly, his attention was distracted by the sound of a blunt object tapping against the window. The tint on the window was dark so he could barely see out of it. All he could see was a silhouette of someone wearing an all-black hoodie and holding a long silver instrument. The assailant then started firing shots straight through the window and side panels of the truck. His upper body was hit with multiple shots before the gunman fled the scene. When Nicki heard the gunshots, she jumped up and ran to the window. From there, she witnessed the assailant running away from the truck. She ran to the phone and dialed 911. In a state of panic, she tried to wake up Leaf while screaming to the operator.

"Help me, please, Leaf, I think they shot your little brother! Wake up! Operator, there's been a shooting. Please send help to Overbrook Park Apartments . . . please hurry! Leaf, wake up! They shot Sha'Ron. We need to go out there and check on him!" she screamed.

Leaf suddenly leaned forward and threw up everything in his stomach. It was as if he instantly sobered up. He stood up and identified his surroundings. Next, he questioned Nicki about the accusations she was making.

"Nicki, what the fuck is you talking about my brother got shot? I don't even remember how the fuck I got here. You tripping."

"Leaf! Sha'Ron drove you home from the bar. He took your truck, and when he left, somebody shot at him and ran. We need to go outside and help him," she pleaded.

Leaf was confused, but after hearing what Nicki told him, he pulled out his gun and ran out of the apartment. She followed closely behind him. As soon as he got outside, he saw the bullet holes in the windows. The tint prevented them from shattering. When he pulled the door open, he discovered Sha'Ron's limp body stretched out over the passenger seat, covered in blood.

"Aw, shit! No, Sha'Ron! No, man! Please don't die. Fuck! Who did this to you?" he cried. Nicki reacted similarly. The approaching sound of ambulance sirens brought them back to reality. Nicki grabbed the gun from his hand and tucked it in her pants seconds before the ambulance and police turned down the block. The police officer pulled them away from the truck so the paramedics could do their job. When they checked his pulse, they discovered he had a faint heartbeat. Having lost a tremendous amount of blood, if he didn't receive immediate medical attention, he would surely die.

"He's still alive. Let's get him on the stretcher!" one EMT informed his partner who instantly kicked into action. They carefully removed his body, placed him in the back of the ambulance, and sped off to the hospital. Because the truck was now the scene of the crime, they were not permitted to drive it. Nicki was able to persuade one of the responding officers to drive her and Leaf down to the hospital.

During the ride, he contacted his mother and informed her about Sha'Ron's misfortune. She, in turn, contacted Connie, and they all planned to meet up at the University of Pennsylvania Hospital. Once all were gathered in the emergency room, they stormed the information booth, demanding to know Sha'Ron's condition and whereabouts.

"I'm sorry, people, but I cannot give out that information. However, I've contacted the hospital spokesperson, and she informed me that she will be down to speak to you shortly."

As they waited impatiently for her arrival, the questions and suspicions were addressed.

"Ka'Leaf, what happened? Who did this to my baby boy? Where the fuck were you, Ka'Leaf? I don't understand how you let could have let this happen. Why? Please, God, don't take my baby," Consuela begged the Lord. Connie stood by her side hugging her supportively, while staring at Leaf and his girlfriend with the evilest look she could muster. Consuela started to shiver uncontrollably, urging Connie to take off her sweat jacket and place it over her shoulders.

When the spokesperson finally arrived, she called them into a small room where grieving and counseling brochures were spread across the table.

"I assume that you are all family and friends of Sha'Ron Santana."

Some replied yes, while others nodded their heads in agreement.

"I've been informed that the doctor is on his way down to give you all a full report on Mr. Santana's status."

"Is he okay? Please tell me he's going to be all right," Consuela pleaded with the nurse.

"I'm sorry, but I don't know his status, ma'am."

The moment the doctor walked through the door, all hope and prayers were denied. The doctor's facial expressions said it all. He appeared sad and disappointed. Informing families that their loved ones were dead was very difficult, but it was his job.

"I'm very sorry, but his vitals were far too low for me to revive him. He didn't make it."

Consuela let out a scream so loud that it could be heard throughout the hospital. The news was too disturbing for her, and she passed out right there on the floor. Everyone present cried their hearts out for Sha'Ron. This was the most painful loss they'd ever experienced. From that day forward, things were never to be the same again. It was as though when Sha'Ron died, he took bits and pieces of everyone's soul along with him.

The following morning in the Federal Detention Center, the block officer woke Gus up and informed him that the jail chaplain sent for him. Confused about why the chaplain wanted to meet with him, he questioned the officer to make sure that it wasn't a mistake.

"You sure he sent for Gustavo Santana?"

"I'm positive. Now put your uniform on and report to the officer station." After being escorted to the chaplain's office, he was offered a seat and a glass of water.

"Mr. Santana. I hate to be the bearer of bad news, but unfortunately, your cousin Sha'Ron Santana was murdered in his car last night. May the Lord have mercy on his soul and your loved ones. I will lead you in prayer if you wish. Do you think that will help you deal with this?" asked the chaplain.

Gus didn't respond. His face went blank, and his skin complexion grew pale. It was as if his heart stopped beating, and he lost the ability to comprehend. The initial shock delayed his ability to come to terms with reality. He stood up and left the office. He was escorted back to the block where he went straight to his cell and lay in his bunk. He buried his face in the pillow and mourned his cousin's death. When Kalid walked in and noticed him crying, he tried to comfort him.

"I seen the news this morning, and I assume the Santana kid was related to you. It seems as if Allah is putting trials and tribulations in your life like never before. I'm not sure if you realize it, but you're in a fucked-up situation with these feds. They give a nigga a million years like it ain't shit. You got to take the time to weigh out your options and do what's best for you and your family," he advised. This was his first attempt to test the waters. When he had contacted his agents earlier that morning, they informed him that if he got Gus to talk and reveal anything about his case or cooperate, he would be given an additional time reduction at sentencing.

Had Gus been on point, he would have recognized Kalid's angle. But since he was experiencing grief and hardship due to the events taking place in his life, he was extremely gullible. He listened closely to every word that was said. He didn't comment on what he suspected Kalid was recommending. Instead, he just prayed that he would be granted a bail at his hearing scheduled for the next day.

The news of Sha'Ron's death was a shock for Black. What was even more surprising was the fact that Colt had somehow made a mix-up, and killed the wrong Santana brother. Over the years, he'd been reliable in his field of work and always demonstrated professionalism. Black couldn't understand what went wrong, and he demanded an explanation. Mysteriously, Colt had not reached out to him. Usually after doing a hit for him, he would confirm that the job was a success, but Black was still waiting.

Meanwhile, Black was also waiting for word on where the funeral services were going to be held. He had every intention of attending.

From Hopeful to Hopelessness

The following day, Gus was led to the courtroom by U.S. Marshals. He was seated beside his attorney, Ryan McMonagle, who quickly briefed him on what he planned to argue.

"Gus, I know you are losing your mind over in that damn rat trap. I've been informed of your losses, and my deepest condolences go out to you and your family. I'm going to do everything in my power to get you bail, but it's not going to be easy. This prosecutor, Joe Khann, is tough as nails, plus he is being backed by an asshole with a lot of pull around here. They are all back there staring at you like you're fresh meat."

"Just do your best to get me out of here, please, man. I need to get back to my family," Gus pleaded.

After two hours of back-and-forth arguments, the prosecution reaped the victory. He was able to convince the judge that Gus was a danger to the community, a flight risk, and likely to continue criminal activities if he was free. The prosecution didn't give specifics, but they did mention to the judge that very serious charges were in the process of being filed. As partial victory for the defense, the judge rescheduled another bail hearing in thirty days. He warned the prosecutor that if serious charges weren't filed, he would consider setting bail.

All of Gus's hopes were thrown out the window. His beliefs and strength were at an all-time low. The disappointment and failure were evident in his expression. Ryan noticed the weakness being exposed and quickly tried to gather him together before the feds smelled it on him.

"You keep your head up in there, Gus. I'll keep fighting to the very end, but you have to stay strong. If anybody other than me should try to contact you, refuse it and contact me immediately." Ryan's voice was loud enough for the agents in the back of the courtroom to hear it. After the hearing, Gus was taken to the holding cells where inmates are held until the marshal transported them back to the jail.

Sha'Ron's *janasa* (Muslim funeral) was to be held at Sister Carra Muhmad's Masjid in West Philly. Before the funeral, his body had to be properly cleansed. This was carried out by Leaf and a few brothers from the masjid who volunteered to assist. When the sheet was removed from his brother's body, not only was he brought back to reality that his baby brother was really gone, but to witness the actual wounds he was inflicted with replaced his heart with an icebox. The sad thing was, there was nothing he could do to help or bring him back. He was gone forever. The fact that everyone was placing the blame on him put him in an awkward position. They washed him off with black soap while praying over his body. He was then wrapped up in a shroud and placed in a box.

The following day, close to five hundred people showed up to pay their final respects. Sha'Ron was deeply loved by many, and in his memory, a river of tears filled the ranks of the masjid. No one's cries were louder than his mother's. She screamed as if she was in agonizing pain.

When people tried to comfort her, she just pushed them away. During the final prayer, Leaf happened to look over to his side and notice that Black prayed directly next to him. At that moment, he was overcome with several bad vibes. A voice in his head was telling him to pull his gun off of his waist and blow the nigga's head off. The only thing that stopped him was the fact that he didn't want to put any more hardship on his mother. After the prayer was completed, Black walked over to Consuela and gave his condolences.

She spat dead in his face and turned her back on him. He stood there in disbelief, wiping the spit from his face. Leaf witnessed the whole incident and made a mental note to question his mother on what was said to make her respond the way she did.

After the burial was complete, everyone went their separate ways except for Connie. She stood at her nephew's grave, praying and talking to him as if he could hear and respond. When she finally left, she headed over to Nicki's apartment. She wanted to know exactly what she heard and saw the night her nephew was killed.

Consuela had always been the quiet one out of the two sisters, but she was not as naïve as people painted her out to be. Unknown to most, she had a dark side as well. Over the years, she had learned to contain it, but now she had all the reason in the world to bring it out. She was almost certain that Black was responsible for her son's death. It was how he got down.

She'd been getting a bad vibe from Black lately, and when he came up to her at the funeral, her mother's intuition told her he knew more than he was letting on. No one besides him would have the courage to shed Santana blood, knowing what the repercussions would be. Since he was shot while sitting in his brother's car gave her reason to believe that the bullets were meant for Leaf, but mistaken identity took place, which led to her baby being killed. When he tried to send his condolences after the service, the nigga couldn't even look her in the eyes, which gave her even more reason to suspect Black. She had knowledge of who his hit man was and planned to get the ultimate vengeance on everyone who participated in her son's demise. She just needed to get her facts straight and line up all her ducks in a row.

Immediately following Gus's hearing, federal agents and prosecutors held a meeting to discuss the progress made and where the investigation needed to go before the rest of the suspects were indicted. Amy led the discussion.

"Throughout our investigations, we have been able to gather a significant amount of evidence and intelligence on mainly all suspects of interest. Our informant and his recording devices have been our most essential resource. The suspects could be heard on numerous recordings discussing their roles in the drug trade, shootings, money laundering, and even murders. Just recently, our informant was able to plant a recording device in the home of our prime suspect, in which we believe we overheard him ordering the murder of Ka'Leaf Santana. We believe that Sha'Ron Santana was not the intended target. He just happened to be at the wrong place at the wrong time. I personally feel that this investigation is at its final stages, and we should get our informant off of the street and round the suspects up," she voiced.

"Thank you, Amy. I agree with you 100 percent. However, I would like to delay this at least one more week. Reason being, I want to pick up a little more conversation from Mr. Campbell and also give another informant we have on the inside an opportunity to encourage Gustavo

Santana to cooperate or talk. I want this case to be solid, and I strongly believe that either of our resources will assure that within another week," he argued.

"One more week it is then, Joe. Now, I have to figure out a way to get our informant away from the suspects long enough to brief him on the issues. I'll figure something out. Until then, let's get our asses back out there and conclude this investigation!" yelled Adam, giving the agents the motivation they needed to work hard, and hopefully bring the matter to closure.

Rat Bastard!

Black had just finished taking his frustrations out during rough sex with Chyna, when the housekeeper, Ms. Rosa, urgently knocked on the door. She had been his housekeeper for the past seven years and had never interrupted him while he was in his bedroom, especially while he was entertaining his wife. Black realized that it had to be an emergency, so he slid on shorts and stepped into the hallway to address the issue.

"Rosa, what the hell is going on? You come banging on the door like a damn madwoman."

"No . . . no . . . Mr. Black, you do not understand. I find something very suspicious. You must come now," she demanded with her Spanish accent, while grabbing his hand to lead him downstairs to the living room. She placed her index finger to her lips and lifted the pillow up. She pointed to the device that she had come across while doing her weekly cleaning. Black stared at it in disbelief while a hundred thoughts ran through his mind. He was all too familiar with these devices. Before his first indictment dropped, he used to have a retired private investigator come to his house and sweep it for bugs on a weekly basis. He deeply regretted abandoning that practice. He had put his guard down and grown too comfortable. Now his empire was in great danger. He knew exactly who was responsible for the device finding its way under the pillows of his couch. His thoughts went back to the other day, when he and Gus had stepped out back.

When they returned, Jihad was acting quite nervous. Now it was clear why. *How the fuck was I so blind? I let this little rat motherfucka jeopardize my whole empire. I'm slipping. I got to fix this shit before it's too late,* he reasoned with himself.

Payback's a Bitch, Literally!

As Colt was exiting his home, he was met by the murderous eyes and the barrel of a gun held by Consuela Santana. She backed him up into the house. Her demands were very clear and simple.

"Keep your hands above your motherfuckin' head! If you even blink hard, I'ma blow your brains out! You understand me?" she stated, clearly in control of the situation. When she reached for his waist, he attempted to smack the gun from her hand. She quickly stepped back and fired a shot into his chest. He hit the ground, wailing with excruciating pain. She stood over him and pressed her foot forcefully against his bullet wound. He started to choke and scream in submission.

"Now, you got one time only to tell me the truth. Did Black order the death of my child?" Knowing what he was accused of and the extent of his injuries, he knew that the only thing he had coming was death. He had no plans of making it easy on himself or giving her peace of mind, so he began taunting her.

"Bitch, fuck you and your dead-ass son! I hope I see the little bastard in hell so I can tell him how much of a whore you are. Fuck you." His words were chilling and suicidal. Consuela stared him straight in the eye and fired several shots into his head. As far as she was concerned, he had basically admitted that Black had indeed told him to kill her son. At this point, Consuela heard what she wanted to hear, and she was choosing to interpret things however she wanted to. She was looking for any reason to justify her carrying out her intentions with no mercy.

Smiling Faces Tell Lies

Back in the Federal Detention Center, Gus was finally granted access to the telephone. His first call was placed to his wife. After setting up his electronic voice message, the call was connected. There was a brief message informing the party of the inmate's name, telling them that the call was being monitored and recorded, and any three-way calling would result in the call being terminated. They then had to push 5 to accept the call or 7 to block any further calls. When Trish's voice came across the line, he could tell that she'd been crying and waiting impatiently for his call.

"Oh my God, Gus, baby, what is going on? Why am I just hearing from you? I miss you so much, baby. I'm scared to death out here, Gus. Everything went haywire after you got locked up. I don't know what to do."

"Only thing we can do is hold on and hope I get bail in thirty days. I don't like to hear you like this. How are you, Mom, and Aunt Consuela holding up?"

"That's the thing, Gus, we ain't holding up! The man of the family is in jail. Those people is trying to take the house, the car, and any other assets we have. You need to do something. We falling apart."

"This shit is fucking crazy. I don't understand none of these charges. I ain't get caught with shit but money, and they talking about some drugs and guns."

"You have one minute remaining. . . ."

"Gus, please call me back whenever you can. I put three hundred dollars on your books. Please take care of yourself in there. I love you, baby," she cried before the phone disconnected. Gus sighed stressfully before hanging up the phone. As he walked back to his cell, he was approached by a bald Muslim man with a long beard.

"What's up, youngin'? Ay, listen, Black is family to me and he sent word to me asking me to look out for you and make sure you was good. I never disappoint my family and friends. The name is Shabazz, and my first lookout is me telling you to move out of that cell with that vicious rat-ass nigga. He hotter than fish grease. That nigga will do anything to go home, so don't talk about your case. I got a bag of food and toiletries for you. Don't take any shit from that rat. Come get the bag before lockdown time."

After the block got locked down for the night, Gus put the items from Shabazz in his locker. While doing so, he stared at Kalid with a twisted-up face. When Kalid took noticed, he inquired about the look.

"Damn, brother, did I do something wrong to you? If looks could kill, I would be dead on sight, right now."

"I tell you what's wrong. Niggas telling me you a rat and you hop on niggas' cases. I hope you don't plan on doing that shit to me because if so, you putting yourself and your family in a fucked-up predicament. My last name Santana, and my niggas on the street will do whatever to make sure I'm secure. You dig me?" he snapped.

Kalid stood up and challenged Gus's words with some of his own.

"Not that it is any of your business, because for real, I don't owe you or any of these other chumps on the block an explanation. Only person who could punish or reward me for my actions is Allah. But, since you so concerned about my situation, yeah, I went in. The Quran says, 'Speak the truth, even when it's against yourself.' I cooperated on my case and told them what I did and what I seen. Nothing more. I ain't never and *will* never hop on another nigga's case." Kalid pounded on his chest, "Believe me, I got my own drama. These niggas in here talking about I'm foul because my codefendants is Muslim, and I turned them over to the oppressors. But when we was out there robbing, killing, selling drugs, and shooting shit up, we wasn't Muslims; we was oppressing the people in our communities. These niggas come to jail and get righteous but was living foul and shysty on the streets. They the ones that's confused, not me. Dealing with these feds, you can either save your face or your ass, but you can't save both. These niggas talk to talk, but deep down inside, they wish they was me. They wish they had something of significance to go in on. How many niggas you know in this day and time that will take thirty years on the chin, knowing they could go in and get five or less? I'm owning mines," he empathized. The look on Gus's face was like that of a child who had just been checked or schooled about the facts of life.

Kalid was relieved when he saw Gus's response. The investigators had promised to put some credit on his commissary and get him his own leather-bound Quran if was able to get information out of Gus, and he was determined to do just that. Seeing how Gus soaked up everything he said, all he had to do now was wait patiently for the opportunity to present itself . . . tactics of a true rat.

Gus lay in his bunk and stayed up all night pondering over all of the decisions and actions he'd been making over that past few months. He was all fucked up thinking about Sha'Ron too. He couldn't believe his little cousin was dead. He felt like he should've been there to protect him. Family was everything to him, and now it seemed like everybody and everything was falling apart. One way or another, he had to figure out how he was going to sort this mess out.

Ready or Not,
Here They Come

Crash!

"FBI! Everybody get on the ground now!" ordered the FBI agents that stormed through Gus's house. The occupants were pulled from their beds where they slept, dressed with practically nothing on. They were gathered on the living room floor where they were searched, cuffed, and made aware of what was happening.

"This property and everything in it is being seized by the United States Government. At this time, you will be escorted off the premises, uncuffed, and free to go as you please. I warn you that this property will be searched thoroughly, and anything illegal will be accounted for. Agents will be here around the clock, so I advise you not to come back or you will be arrested for trespassing.

"Take them out of here."

Connie, Trish, and Jihad were escorted off the property in nightgowns and underwear. Once the cuffs came off, Connie started her performance. She cussed the agents out and made insulting accusations.

"You motherfuckas couldn't wait to take that house. Jealous mafuckas. Y'all just mad my son was living better than you at half your age. But guess what? There's plenty more where that came from. As long as they make money, us Santanas going to find a way to get it." Jihad and Trish had to literally pull her down the block to avoid being arrested for disturbing the peace.

Luckily, Connie had prepared for the raid and was ten steps ahead of them. From past experience, she knew that there was a great possibility that the feds would come to seize all of Gus's assets in the wake of his indictment. As a precaution, the other day, she packed a duffle bag with her money and guns and placed it in the trunk of the BMW. She had parked the car around the corner from the house. She went to the stash spot where she retrieved the spare set of keys she had hidden. Temporary relief set in as they drove away from the area.

Leaf paced back and forth in his living room, anxious to receive some news he'd been waiting on. His mother had confided in him that she thought Black was responsible for Sha'Ron's death. She told him she was pretty sure that the bullets were meant for him. He'd been waiting to hear from his mother all evening. She had promised to come by tonight and give him more information.

"Leaf!" Consuela burst through the front door. "I took care of the motherfucka that did that to my baby. It was definitely Black's orders. I took out the shooter, so I'm trusting you to take care of that snake motherfucker Black. But before you do, I got some other shit I gotta take care of. I'll call you when it's time to take that nigga out," she instructed. "If for some reason I can't call you, keep your ear to the street. When they start talking, shut them the fuck up. Don't let me or your brother down. You better make that nigga pay for what he did," she barked before grabbing Leaf and embracing him as if it was the last time.

As she was leaving, she bumped into Nicki who was returning home from work. At first, Nicki thought it was

Connie coming to harass her with a hundred questions again, but at closer look, she recognized it was Consuela. She looked like she hadn't slept in days. She was still wearing the same black sweat jacket that Connie had put over her shoulders at the hospital the night Sha'Ron was killed. They stopped and greeted each other briefly.

"How you coming along, Consuela?"

"I'm heartbroken, Nicki. I miss my baby boy." Consuela took a deep breath, "But I'll be all right." Suddenly, she looked at her watch and discovered the time.

"Shit, I gotta go. I don't want to miss this bitch," she stated before bolting out of the apartment and running to her Range Rover.

Nicki stared on, feeling sorry for her and her family. As she watched Consuela run off, an image came to mind. She suddenly gasped and brought her hands to her mouth. *Oh my God. Please tell me I'm wrong. God, don't let it be true.*

She couldn't believe what she had just come to realize. She was tempted to go and tell Leaf immediately what she'd just discovered, but she decided to get her thoughts and words together before saying anything. The last thing she wanted to do was start more drama. She needed to get her facts together before she said anything at all to Leaf. She was nervous, anxious, and scared of what was going to happen if she revealed what she'd just come to realize. Nicki felt her heart racing and her palms sweating. Beads of sweat started to form on her forehead, and her stomach was in knots. Before she had a chance to run toward the Dumpster, she threw up her dinner all over the parking lot.

The Cleanup

After analyzing the situation over and over again, Black decided it was time to take action. The demise of the Santana family was the only chance he had of coming out on top. He had already reached out to his boy Shabazz that was in the same detention center as Gus. Shabazz had assured him that he would keep a close eye on Gus. But Black now needed his man to do more. Shabazz had just gotten thirty years for a robbery, and Black was confident that once he reached out and offered him six figures to leave Gus stinking, that he'd be delighted to move out for the cause. Ryan was scheduled to pay him an attorney visit later that evening and offer the proposal.

As for Jihad, Black had something special planned for his ass. What Jihad had done was unforgivable. He had to be dealt with under special circumstances. Black took his deceitful actions very personal. He had violated him and his home in the worst way imaginable. He vowed that he would personally demonstrate how to deal accordingly with a rat.

Later on that evening, Ryan McMonagle entered the lobby of the Federal Detention Center. At the visiting booth, he passed the officer his government-issued attorney license and waited for her to inspect it.

"Who will you be seeing today, Mr. McMonagle?" she inquired after verifying his identification.

"Stanly Smith, please, ma'am," he responded. The officer pointed to an attorney booth and informed him his visitor would be down shortly. After a ten-minute wait, Stanly Smith, aka Shabazz, walked into the booth with a confused expression on his face. Ryan recognized it immediately and quickly apologized for the inconvenience.

"I'm sorry for the unexpected visit, but something very urgent has come up. Black is very confident that you will be able to assist him in the matter. To assure you of that, he's prepared to give you one hundred thousand dollars. This Santana kid has become a headache and you know Black hates Tylenol. So, what's your take on this one, Shabazz?"

He didn't respond right away as he contemplated the matter with great consideration. When he finally spoke, he stared Ryan directly in his eyes.

"It's no question that I'm qualified to take care of the matter. When they gave me thirty mafuckin' years, they took my life as I used to know it. This *is* my life. So, now that I've got nothing to lose and everything to gain, I'ma handle the little nigga with pleasure, but I need paper up front. Take my sister's address and phone number down, and drop it off to her tonight. She hip. I'll call her in the morning and get confirmation. Once that happens, y'all will have a receipt in the form of a death certificate. Tell Black I send my best wishes, and it's always a pleasure doing business with him. I probably be in the hole for a couple of years, but I'm a soldier. As long as my peoples is comfortable, I'ma be comfortable. Here's her info. Well, you got work to do, and so do I, so let's not hold each other up any longer," he suggested before standing up. After they shook hands to seal the deal, they both went their separate ways.

***

Consuela was in such a rush to get to the day care center, she almost crashed into the back of a trash truck. Once she finally made it there, she was relieved to spot Chyna's Mercedes still parked out back. She parked her Range Rover close by. While she patiently waited, she pulled the .45 Beretta from her waist and stroked the powerful instrument as if it were some sort of pet. Ever since she found out that Chyna owned this particular day care center, she'd been stationed there every day. Through her observation, she discovered that Chyna's daughter attended the school as well. Today, she planned to even the score. She was a firm believer of getting shit even with people. An eye for an eye and a tooth for a tooth has always been her way of thinking. With Black having killed her son, nothing was off-limits as far as she was concerned. She was looking forward to what was about to come next. But something unexpected took place that put a delay in her plans. When Chyna exited the establishment, Consuela crouched down to make sure Chyna didn't see her. Consuela was a little perplexed when she realized Chyna was by herself, though. She was expecting Chyna to be with her and Black's daughter. She figured someone else must have picked up the little girl earlier that day.

"Bitch, you lucked up today. Go on home to your bitch-ass husband, walking around this motherfucker like your shit don't stink. You and your husband are filthy, stinking motherfuckers. Best believe I'ma be here bright and early tomorrow and every other day until I get my motherfuckin' payback," she promised.

After dropping the hundred thousand dollars off at Shabazz's sister's house, Black headed over to Gus's spot. He drove a white van with a paint company logo

on the side. He brought along the proper accessories
to assist him in the murderous plot: plastic, gasoline,
power saw, and shovel. Since this was a personal matter, he brought out his personal guns, including his twin
Glock 40s with the silencers attached, an AK-47, and a
hunting knife. He shaved all the hair off of his head and
wore a Dickies overalls suit. He had pulled his daughter
out of school earlier that day to spend some quality time
with her. At the rate shit was going, tomorrow was far
from promised for him. However it went, this was the
life he chose. Ratting wasn't an option, nor was crying.
Too bad he couldn't say the same for the people in his
circle. Because of that, he wasn't taking any chances. As
he drove, the voice of the legendary Sam Cooke cranked
through the speakers, providing the motivational music
to give him the extra push and reminder of what needed
done.

*"It's been a long time, a long time coming, but I know
a change gonna come. Oh, yes it will. It's been too hard
living, but I'm afraid to die, 'cause I don't know what's
up there, beyond the sky . . ."*

When he drove down Gus's block, he bumped into yet
another surprise. The alphabet boys were present. Their
cars were parked around the house, and they could be
seen walking in and out of the front door.

"What the fuck! Did that rat-ass nigga get Connie
locked up too? I got to find where they hiding this pussy
at. There ain't enough hours in a day for this shit," he
cursed as he continued to drive with no specific destination in mind.

All Eyes on Me

Now that Gus was in jail, Leaf finally felt like he could breathe a little more easily. All his life he'd felt like he was walking in his cousin's shadow. It was finally his time to shine. Now, niggas had no choice but to deal with him. There were a few niggas in the city still making moves on their own, but as of late, he and his crew had shit on smash. The money, power, and respect combined had the nigga feeling like a king.

The only thing that was bringing him sadness was that he didn't have his brother standing next to him. He felt guilty that his brother had taken bullets meant for him, and he had been losing a lot of sleep over it. He wanted everyone involved to pay for what they did to Sha'Ron. He had been waiting on his mother's call to make his move, and he was running out of patience. His mother had exactly one day to take care of whatever "business" she was referring to; then he was unleashing the beast.

Outside of his business and revenge plans, he had been thinking about making some changes in his love life too. He had decided to make him and Nicki official once he'd taken care of shit and things calmed down a little bit. She had been extrasupportive during his unfortunate times and demonstrated enormous patience in dealing with him. The way she'd been handling herself since the night of his brother's shooting showed how loyal she was. She was a ride or die, and she'd always told him that all she had ever wanted in return was love and quality time. He was supposed to be moving into a furnished condo the following morning, and he had already told her that he wanted her to come with him. As much as he loved his current spot, it was obvious his enemies knew where he rested his head, so he had no intentions on staying around. He couldn't wait for all this shit to blow over so he could chill at his new spot with his feet up like a king, while his team maintained control and played their positions to the fullest.

Nicki had requested some weed earlier that evening so he called Ikeal and told him to bring some exotic, along with a few bottles of syrup. His man stopped everything he was doing to accommodate him and come right through for him. As he and Nicki puffed on the exotic weed, they blasted 50 Cent old shit from *Get Rich or Die Tryin'*. Fuck the neighbors. It was their last night there anyway, they reasoned. Leaf had drunk two bottles of syrup like it wasn't about nothing. The codeine and weed made the nigga horny as hell, not to mention the way Nicki's ass was jiggling in those tight-ass booty shorts while she danced to the music. The weed always seemed to loosen her right up.

Pulling her to him, he directed her head to the area that urged for oral attention. She went straight to work. As he lit up another Dutch, he lay back and enjoyed the warm, wet, soft insides of her mouth. The way she was able to make his entire nine inches disappear in the back of her mouth made him choke on the weed and caused his body to jerk from excitement. Going the extra length to please her man, she gently licked all over his balls while giving him a hand job at the same time. Afterward, she then took turns with his balls, placing them in her mouth one at a time and sucking on them with just her lips. He grabbed the back of her ponytail and pulled it with just enough force to balance the pleasure she had him feeling.

Wanting to show her that he could fulfill her with just as much pleasure, he stood up and switched positions. Her shorts were so tight that he had great difficulty getting them down. He refused to let them slow down his hunger and craving, so he gripped the side slits and ripped them off. The sight of her bald, clean-smelling pussy caused his mouth to water. He pushed her legs up and guided her arms around them so that they stayed held apart. Then he started talking dirty.

"Hold these mafucking legs open, girl. You hear me? You let them go, I'ma smack you across your ass so hard, my fingerprints going to be left behind. You hear me? Now, watch me as I fuck you with my tongue," he whispered. He started off by licking from the top of her pussy lips to the bottom of her asshole. At first he went fast, and then drastically slowed up, until it was as if he was moving in slow motion. The pleasure was too much for her to bear, causing her legs to release from her grip. As promised, he smacked her ass with force, only adding pain to her pleasure. She quickly readjusted the position. This time, he spread her lips apart and flicked his tongue in and out of her pussy as if it was a snake. He was able to push his thumbs up on the sides of her pussy and cause her clit to be fully exposed. He kissed it with loud, long smooches that sent a vibrant current down her spine. Her body started to shiver as if she had the chills. The orgasm was so explosive that it actually squirted out like a water gun. Leaf's face was covered in her juices, but it was far from over.

"Come sit on top and make me do what you just did," he suggested.

Following his wishes, she sat on top and bounced on him like there was no tomorrow. She had to hold both of her titties to prevent them from smacking against her body too hard. When she started winding her body from side to side, that was all it took. He bust up all inside her.

The sex was great and tiring. They fell asleep in their last position. Nicki's plans to share her secret would have to wait for another day. After building up enough courage to expose the scandalous act, good pipe done postponed it once again.

When the Hunter Gets Contacted by the Prey

Just when Black thought all hope was lost, he received a phone call that put him right back on course.

"Black, are you busy right now? I really need your help," pleaded Connie.

"Busy? Shit, I been busy all night. But if I can assist you with something, I can stop what I'm doing. What's up?"

"First of all, I want to apologize on behalf of my sister. I saw what she did at the funeral. She's just going through it right now. I know you ain't have shit to do with the death of my nephew. But anyway, I got some troubles with them alphabet folks, and we got put out of our own fucking house. They really fucked up my living arrangement. They didn't let us get shit; they kicked us out in our bed clothes. We got plenty of money but no identification, so we can't get no hotel room. Let us lay up in one of your spots just for the night, please," she insisted.

"I can do that for y'all. It's just you, Jihad, and Trish, right?"

"Yeah, it's just us."

"Where y'all at right now?"

"We at Friday's on City Line Avenue, waiting on our food."

"All right, that's cool. Meet me down at my apartment complex on Fortieth and Market in an hour, and I'ma look out for y'all," he reassured her. Black exhaled a deep breath of relief. He couldn't believe his luck. Connie had no idea she had just set herself up. He had no intentions of letting the opportunity escape him. If he had anything to do with it, they weren't going to make it out of Friday's parking lot.

I just hit the fucking jackpot! This shit is almost going to be too easy, he thought to himself as he got ready to head out.

After chowing down on their meals and a few drinks, the threesome exited the establishment and headed for the car. Once they were inside, Connie allowed the car to heat up while adjusting the radio to her favorite classical station, 105.3. Suddenly, the passenger-side window shattered, and Jihad leaned over Connie's lap, bleeding from his head. In a state of panic, she threw the car into reverse as silent, deadly, hot metals continued to fly through the doors and windows of the car. In a desperate attempt to escape, she ended up ramming the car into a light pole. For a split second, she wished that her gun was in her hand and not the trunk. Her flesh started to burn, and she felt extremely light-headed. The only reason she didn't pass out was because Trish's screams were loud and directly in her ear. With her last bit of strength, she managed to cut the wheel, put the car in drive, and give it gas. This enabled them to escape the direct line of fire. When she made it to the exit of the parking lot, she could not make the left turn because Jihad's body was still slumped over her lap and his head had slid directly under the steering wheel. As she was attempting to move his body, the car was hit from behind with so much force that it flew into the intersection of City Line Avenue's busy traffic, colliding with a SEPTA bus and another car.

As Black sped away in the opposite direction, he was semisatisfied with the results. Things happened so fast, he had to replay the entire event in his head to get a clear picture of what happened. He remembered stepping out of the van the second he spotted them exiting the restaurant. From behind a nearby bush, he got a clear visual of the car. His main objective was to kill Jihad first. His first shot was trained at his temple, which he executed with perfect marksmanship. With both guns in hand, he rained down on the car as it attempted to escape. He was certain that his gunfire hit everyone in the car. If, for some odd reason, their gunshot wounds weren't life threatening, then the head-on collision with the bus was likely to seal the deal.

Knowing it was a possibility that the feds would somehow become aware they were supposed to meet up that night, he parked the van up in a garage and drove another car down to Fortieth and Market Street. He waited until the hour was up, plus an additional ten minutes before he started calling Connie's phone. Her phone went straight to voice mail. He decided to leave a message.

"Yo, Connie, you got me down at Fortieth Street waiting on you. I told you I had shit to do so if you ain't here in the next ten minutes, I'm out." He called back ten minutes later to inform her that he was leaving.

"Connie, you full of shit. If you wasn't coming, you could have at least called me and told me you was good. You ain't have to cut your mafuckin' phone off. I'm out," he snapped. Now that he had covered his ground as best he could, he headed home. That night, Black felt such a peace deep within, that he slept like a baby. It had been a few days since he'd been able to get some decent sleep and rest. He took full advantage and decided he would sleep in the following morning.

***

When police and paramedics arrived at the scene of the accident, they were surprised to see that dozens of federal agents had beaten them there. The car had sustained severe damage and had to be cut open with the Jaws of Life before they could attend to the victims. After twenty minutes of cutting, they were finally able to pull the victims from the wreckage. The male passenger was pronounced dead on the scene, and the two females were rushed to the hospital in serious condition. When it was revealed that the victims of the car accident were part of an ongoing investigation, the federal agents rushed in and took over immediately.

They would not permit Jihad's body to be removed. He was considered federal property; therefore, he would be handled by their own people. They were clearly upset about him being killed on their watch. Someone would surely have to answer for it and be reprimanded. While searching the car for evidence, they stumbled upon cell phones, a duffle bag full of money, and a silver nine-millimeter handgun. After the items were recorded, labeled, and packaged, they were taken straight to the lab to be examined.

Thin Line between Sleep and Death

Around the same time, over at the Federal Detention Center, Shabazz was still wide awake. He spent the majority of the night sharpening the point of his knife with a piece of sandpaper and a nail file. Once he finished, the point was so sharp, when he tapped it with his index finger, it drew blood. Afterward, he packed up all his legal material, pictures, and toiletries, preparing to be placed in administrative segregation.

Once the morning arrived, he kept close tabs on 507 cell. Neither of them got up for breakfast, and they still remained sleeping in bed. At 6:00 a.m., the phone system finally turned on. He called his sister up to see if everything was official. She answered and quickly accepted the charges.

"Ay, sis, what's good? You still love me or what?" which in code meant, *Did you get the money?*

"Boy, for the hundredth time, yes, I love you. We all love you." Not only did she confirm that the money had been dropped off, but when she said, *for the hundredth time,* that also confirmed that the amount was a hundred thousand. After finishing up his conversation, he was prepared to live up to his end of the bargain.

Once he made his way to the cell, he quietly pulled the door open and stepped in. Walking over to the bunk, he stood directly on the side of Gus. Because he slept on his side, it made things a little complicated, prohibiting him from striking the vital areas. He quickly solved the problem by pulling him out of the bed and stabbing him repeatedly in the chest. Gus lifted his arms to his upper body, hoping to avoid the more serious injuries to his chest. Woken up by the commotion and realizing what was going on, Kalid jumped out of bed and attempted to intervene. When he tried to grab Shabazz's hand, he was caught with a left-hand hook that sent him crashing into the wall. In that one split second, Gus managed to crawl out of the cell in view of the block officer. Seeing that the inmate was covered in blood, he pushed deuces on his walkie-talkie. This sent the signal to every officer in the building to respond to the fifth floor.

Meanwhile, back in the cell, Shabazz intended to make Kalid pay dearly for interfering in his business and fucking up his kill. He stabbed him in the chest, head, and neck. He stopped stabbing only when he stopped moving. Hearing the officers storming the block, he flushed the knife down the toilet and tried to wash the blood from his hands. The officers threw a smoke bomb into the cell and fired several rubber bullets. After a five-minute standoff, Shabazz finally surrendered. When the officers entered the cell, they discovered a gruesome scene. There was so much blood splattered on the walls and floors that it resembled a slaughterhouse. Kalid was unresponsive to the officers that did a preliminary examination on him. Both injured inmates were placed on a stretcher and rushed down to the infirmary. This was one of the worst stabbings the federal building had seen in a while.

Tied Ball Game

They say when it rains it pours, and when this happened in the hood, it was usually referring to the increase of the body count. Death always had the tendency to come in threes, and this morning, Consuela had every intention to keep the superstition alive. By the time Chyna arrived at the day care center, Consuela was already in place and ready to move out. The sun had yet to fully come up. This gave her just enough cover of darkness needed to catch her target by surprise.

After stepping out of her car, Chyna opened the back door and proceeded to unfasten the seat belt from her daughter's child safety seat. She was suddenly startled from the shadow that appeared directly behind her. She quickly turned to confront the stalker and came face-to-face with Consuela. She appeared distressed and disoriented. She had on the same clothes that she wore at her son's funeral. Her hair was unkempt, and her eyes had a crazed look to them. Curious to what the unexpected visit was about, Chyna questioned her motives.

"Consuela, is everything all right? You scared the living shit out of me walking up behind me like that. Is there something you need to talk to me about? You not having no affair with my husband, are you?" Evidently, she didn't take notice of the gun she held in her hand. A slight smile appeared on Consuela's face before she responded to the accusations.

"This *is* about your husband. I would say I'm sorry for what I'm about to do, but that would make me a liar. Say good-bye to your baby, bitch!" she spat before shoving Chyna to the side.

Bocka! Bocka! Bocka! Bocka! All four shots hit the child in the head. The poor child never stood a chance. As soon as Chyna regained her footing, she pushed Consuela over and crouched over her daughter's bloody, shot up body.

"My baby!" she wailed. "Not my baby." She grabbed at her daughter's head slumped over and tried to get it to stand straight. Chyna was in a state of disbelief as she attempted to comfort her daughter's lifeless body. Seeing the pain and sorrow in Chyna's face provided Consuela with satisfaction, knowing that she had passed her grief and pain on to her enemies. She wanted them to feel the exact suffering that she felt when she lost her son. It seemed like the longer she stared at Chyna, rocking her daughter in her arms, begging the Lord not to take her away, the more relief she got.

"That's right, bitch. Your man took my baby, and now, I done took yours," Consuela yelled at her as spit flew out of her mouth.

"You killed my baby!" Chyna snapped out of her trance, released her daughter, and charged at Consuela with a crazed look on her face. Before she could even lay a finger on her target, Consuela swiftly raised her weapon and fired the remaining shots into Chyna's chest, neck, and stomach. Her body made a loud thud when it fell onto the concrete. Consuela calmly stepped over the body and fired the remaining bullets straight into Chyna's head. The bullets damaged her face so severely that there wasn't a doctor in the world that could repair her image enough to get her an open casket at her funeral. Certain that there were no survivors or witnesses to the crime, Consuela jumped into her Range and headed to her next destination.

The Aftermath

With the exception of a few minor lacerations and a slightly pierced lung, Gus was in fair condition. He was confined to the infirmary on bed rest for observation and his own protection. On the other hand, Kalid wasn't so lucky. After losing so much blood, he had to be airlifted from the jail and flown to a local hospital. His condition was listed as extremely critical. There weren't too many things in life that Gus didn't have understanding of, or wasn't able to figure out, but the incident that almost cost him his life was one of the few. As much as he hated to acknowledge it, there was no doubt that Black had ordered the hit. Shabazz was Black's peoples who used commissary items and Black's name to gain his trust, claiming that Black told him to look out for him. This made him look at Black in a different way. *This nigga probably was behind getting my cousin killed. I can't believe this shit. That nigga supposed to been like a father to me. What the fuck would make him do this?* he wondered.

As he lay there in denial, his thoughts were interrupted by the jail chaplain and one of the agents who arrested him. Just when he thought things couldn't get any worse, they informed him that there was more disturbing news.

"Son, I don't know what kind of lifestyle you and your family live, but it's catching up in the worst ways imaginable. Just last night, your friend Jihad Cooper was killed, and your mother and wife are fighting for their lives as we speak. To make matters worse, someone tried to kill you in this very facility. I'm starting to believe you have an omen on you."

"Wait! You said *what?* My wife and my mother? Don't tell me no shit like that, man. No! This can't be real, man. What the fuck is going on out there?"

"If I may cut in, I'm sure you remember me from the other day." Adam stepped forward and leaned in toward Gus. "Again, I'm the federal agent supervising over your case. I'm not going to bullshit you. I've been to the hospital, talked with the doctors, and they believe that your mother is going to make a full recovery. But your wife, she is in real bad shape. We have our suspicions of who is responsible for this, but, of course, no one's going to come forward so the suspect is probably going to walk. This may be a surprise to you, but your friend Jihad Cooper was working for us. We actually got him out of jail for the sole purpose of having him work for us. You were our original target, but we shifted the investigation, and we are currently building a case against Curtis 'Black' Campbell. Jihad was our key witness in this whole indictment. Without his testimony, our case against Black is weak.

"Now, since I'm so desperate to get this fucker off the streets, I'm willing to offer you full immunity for the murders and shootings you committed down in South Philly, plus your involvement in this whole drug conspiracy . . . for your cooperation." Adam stopped talking to see if Gus had anything to say. When Gus didn't say anything, he continued. "Look, I'll even go a step further and take you out of jail to go see your wife for an hour or two. What do you say?" asked Adam as he prayed to God that Gus would be willing to cooperate.

Everything was happening too fast, like it was all meant to be. The deal the fed was offering was very tempting, but being a rat wasn't in his nature or character. Even with the snake shit that he suspected Black had done to him and his family weighing on his conscience, he couldn't go against his principles and values. Swallowing the lump in his throat and fighting back the tears, he responded to the fed's offer according to his ethics and the way he was brought up.

"This the life I chose, and I have to live with that. I ain't doing no fucking telling. As a matter of fact, I think I need to contact my lawyer," he stated while trying to conceal his pain and sorrow.

"Lawyer? Oh, you must not have been notified. Mr. McMonagle has resigned from your case as of this morning. You think I would have been able to come within two feet of you with McMonagle still being your lawyer? I wish. But anyway, I'm sorry we couldn't be of more benefit to each other. I tried. Before I leave, let me show you this picture. They sent this over to me this morning. I thought you'd be interested in seeing it," he explained before retrieving it from his inside pocket and laying it facedown on his bed. He shook the chaplain's hand, then turned and walked away.

When Gus picked up the picture to view it, his heart was broken into a million pieces. It showed Trish's body from her stomach up to her face. On her left side, he could clearly see the deformity in the section where her ribs were removed. Her right arm from the elbow down was twice its normal size and covered with bullet holes. There was a tube down her throat, and her eyes were swollen shut. If that wasn't enough, her face was covered in black and blue bruises. All the strength and restraint in the world could not stop the tears from pouring out of his eyes. Seeing his wife stretched out like that touched an unfamiliar side that he didn't know existed.

The fight was over. Defeat had overcome him.

Adam purposely walked away slowly, knowing that once Gus saw the picture, he would reconsider his offer. Had he been a betting man, he would have gambled the house, and indeed, he would have come out a winner. Gus practically screamed and begged for him to return with the same offer.

Over the Edge

Consuela drove straight to Sha'Ron's grave site at Cobbscreek Cemetery. The grave was yet to have a tombstone, and the soil was still fresh. It took all the courage she had left just to walk over to her son's grave. From there, she fell to her knees and began rubbing her hands through the dirt, as if it provided comfort for her son that lay beneath it. Once she found the correct words to say, she voiced her pain and sorrow out loud, believing that he could somehow hear every last word.

"Sha'Ron, my son. My baby, I'm so sorry. I should have never brought you into this lifestyle. I should have never condoned it. Now look where it got you. All the money, cars, and jewelry can't do you no good in here. Baby, you ain't die alone. The mafuckas that did this to you paid the ultimate price . . . every last one of them. But I'm tired, baby . . . real tired. My heart is broken, and the guilt in my soul won't let me rest. I just can't live with myself," she sobbed. She lay on the fresh dirt and cried until she had no tears left.

Afterward, she walked back to the car, picked up her cell phone, and called Leaf. While she waited for him to answer, she loaded the clip to her gun with one bullet.

"Hey, Ma. Where have you been? I've been waiting for you to call me for days," he rambled on without even giving her a chance to speak.

"Listen clearly, Ka'Leaf. It's done. I did what I needed to do. Now you've got the green light to go. You make sure you take care of everything I asked you to. Get a pen and paper so I can give you this nigga's house address."

"Hold on a second, Ma." Leaf moved the phone away from his mouth. "Nicki! Bring me a pen and piece of paper," he instructed his girlfriend.

"All right, Mom, give it to me."

"8701 Bailey Road. It's a few blocks up from the King of Prussia Mall. You got it?" she asked.

"Yea, Ma, I got it."

"Okay. Good. Take care of yourself. Good-bye, Ka'Leaf." Consuela swallowed a lump in her throat. "I love you, son," she expressed before disconnecting the call.

"Mom, you there? Mom, hello!" he yelled into the phone to no avail. She had hung up on him. He tried to call her back several times, but there was no answer. This frustrated him so much that he threw the phone against the wall, breaking it into pieces. Something about that call sent a chill down his spine. Nicki ran to his side to investigate the problem.

"What's wrong, baby? That was your mother, wasn't it? Is she all right?"

"Yeah, that was my mom, but she didn't sound like herself. Something wasn't right about that call," Leaf admitted. He had a weird feeling that he couldn't really understand, but he had shit to take care of so he had to shake it off for now.

"Anyway, I got to go take care of something that might get really dangerous. If I make it out alive, I want us to settle down for a minute. I gave my mom my word I would take care of this, though, so I gotta follow through with it. Hold shit down 'til I get back." As he stood up and prepared to walk away, she grabbed his legs and wrapped her arms around him. She cried hysterically while holding on for dear life. All this emotional shit was starting to get to him. His little brother was dead, his mother wasn't acting like herself, his cousin whom he'd once loved like a brother, was now an enemy, and now his girl was having a breakdown.

"What? What's wrong now? Nicki, I can't handle all this crying and begging. I told you I got some business to take care of. Now, stop all the mafucking crying, get up, and act like you got some sense," he snapped. Nicki couldn't keep her secret in any longer. She knew Leaf was heading over to Black's to kill him. She couldn't let him walk out of that door without him knowing the truth about things. The time was now or never.

"Okay, I'm sorry, but I need you to hear me out, Leaf. Remember the night when your brother got killed? I told you when I heard the gunshots, I ran to the window and saw somebody with a black hoodie running away from the truck. Well, when we got to the hospital and your aunt showed up, I am almost 100 percent certain that she was wearing the same hooded jacket I saw the killer wearing. Then, I thought it was really weird that Connie kept asking me what I saw that night. When I told her I had seen someone running away in a black hoodie, she asked me if I saw the face or car. I answered all of her questions at the hospital. But then she came back a few days later, asking me the same questions all over again. She seemed paranoid as hell, and I thought it was so weird of her."

"Nicki, she was asking questions probably because she wants to get to the bottom of things just like me and moms."

"Yeah, I kept telling myself that too. But, this is what put the icing on the cake. You remember how she gave your mom the hoodie that night at the hospital?"

"Yeah," Leaf nodded, wondering where the hell Nicki was going with all of this.

"Well, when your mom came over the other day, I caught her in the parking lot, and I noticed she was still wearing the same hoodie. As we were talking, she remembered there was something important she had to do, and she suddenly bolted out to her truck. As she ran, I watched her, and a flashback of the killer running away came to my mind. Although the run wasn't the same, the shape was indisputably identical. And who is your mom's identical twin?" Nicki looked at Leaf who sat there with no expression on his face.

The story she presented was nothing more than a story to Leaf because he was in denial. He underestimated that Connie was heartless enough to carry out an execution on her own family. There was no way to be certain the hit was for him or Sha'Ron, and there was no way to be certain of who the killer had really been. Nicki's story did make a little bit of sense, but why hadn't she said anything sooner? There was just too much speculation, uncertainty, for him to say he believed her.

What if Black got her to turn on me, and she's trying to set me up to kill my aunt? What if she's the one that killed my brother that night? How is it that she was the only witness that night? Leaf was suddenly overwhelmed with emotions. His mind was racing, and he felt like he was about to lose it. He stood to his feet, grabbed his head, and just snapped. The little bit of sanity he still possessed instantly went out the window.

Whack! Bam! Boom! Leaf was punching, kicking, and stomping Nicki out.

"Get the fuck up, bitch! What, you fucking that nigga Black? You trying to protect that mafucka, ain't you?" *Whack!* He smacked her again. Smacks turned to punches, and if that wasn't damaging enough, he pulled his gun from his hip and commenced to pistol-whip her severely.

"Leaf, please stop!" Nicki begged him, "Leaf, please!" she said with a mouth full of blood. The more she screamed, the harder he hit her. Before long, she wasn't able to scream at all. The blood from her nose and mouth had prevented her from breathing. She ended up choking to death on her own blood. Leaf was exhausted and collapsed onto the couch, the last images in his head before blacking out were of his mother, Connie, Gus, Black, and Sha'Ron.

Karma Has Come

Around eight o'clock that morning, Rosa came knocking on the door, waking Black from a pleasant dream to a horrific nightmare. Before he allowed himself to snap on Rosa, he took notice that she held the phone out to him and whispered, "Police!"

Believing that it was somehow connected to last night's deadly attacks, he was at first hesitant to accept the call. On second thought, he didn't want them to be under the impression that he had something to hide. Using his better judgment, he took the call.

"Yes, what's this about?"

"This is Homicide Detective Leonard Booker. I've been trying to contact you since a little after six o'clock this morning. Does your wife own First Starter's Preschool in West Philly?"

"Yes, but what does this have to do with you calling my phone at eight o'clock in the morning?" Black asked with concern.

"Let me ask you these two questions before I answer that. Does she own a maroon Mercedes-Benz? And do you have any children?"

"Listen, I don't know what the fuck this is about. But, yes, that's my wife's car, and, yes, we have a daughter together. Now, why does all this concern a homicide detective?"

"Sir, I'm afraid you need to come down to the Philadelphia morgue and identify the two bodies believed to be your wife and daughter. We discovered the bodies, fitting their descriptions, in the parking lot by the maroon Mercedes at the day care center. They were apparently victims of an execution-style killing."

"I don't know how you got this fucking number, but I strongly suggest you stop playing on my fucking telephone. I will have this number traced back to you, find out who you are and where you live, and kill you and everyone you love. You hear me, motherfucker?" he snapped.

"Umm, sir, I understand how difficult this must be for you. It's very difficult just telling you. But if you'll turn to your local news station, you will see for yourself that I speak the truth. Afterward, sir, I urge you to come down to the morgue so that we can get a positive—"

Black slammed the phone down before the man could finish and bolted across the room to the television. As soon as he turned on Channel Seven, he caught the middle of a breaking news story about the day care shootings.

"... *neighbors and coworkers are clueless as to who would want to kill a mother and child in such a malicious manner, outside of a learning center for young children. Parents are outraged and fear it could have been any one of them. One of the parents shared her feelings with Channel 7 Action News.*"

"*I'm just speechless. What kind of person would do something so sick to a child that is three years old? Chyna was the sweetest person you could meet, and her daughter was the most adorable child. I can't understand why anybody would do this. My prayers go out to them.*"

"*Our prayers here at Channel 7 Action News go out to them and their families as well. In other news, a man was killed and two women seriously injured after a gunman opened fire on their car and rammed the back of their vehicle with his, sending them flying into oncoming traffic. There are not many details being mentioned about the victims' identities at this time. Federal authorities have taken full control of that investigation, and we've been told that they are keeping it under wraps. We'll be back with these and more stories making headlines around the city when we return from this commercial break."*

Black was unable to move. He just sat there staring at the television. Reality was too much for him to bear. He couldn't breathe, he couldn't cry, nor could he feel. His philosophy of being a winner regardless of the situation was challenged—and defeated. Feeling like he was a loser was something he couldn't come to terms with. He didn't understand it, never experienced it, nor was he prepared for it. In fact, he had been winning for so long, he believed he was exempt from losing. Life was a bitch, but Karma was a motherfucker. The same acts he terrorized others with over the years came back on him 100 times worse.

Suddenly, a loud crashing sound came from downstairs and snapped him out of the trance. Rosa let out a horrified scream, followed by the eruption of gunshots. Her screams were silenced. Dozens of footsteps could be heard scurrying through the house. They ransacked and invaded rooms downstairs, then made their way up. His mind was temporarily taken away from his personal family issues, and his killer instinct kicked in. He stood up and tiptoed over to the closet where he kept his AK-47 with the drum attached. In his mind, he thought the intruders were those responsible for killing his wife and child. Their footsteps and voices were now directly outside of his bedroom door. Aiming the assault rifle in the direction of the area where they were creeping, he squeezed the trigger, firing a burst of rounds straight through the doors and walls. He heard the thumping sound of at least one intruder hitting the floor before shots were exchanged. It was now an all-out battle. At least forty or fifty shots erupted. The AK-47 was too powerful and equipped with too many shots for the intruders to stick around. When he heard them retreating, he pursued them with caution. Stepping out of his bedroom, he stood over the one who he heard hit the ground. There was a hole in his stomach so big that his intestines were easily exposed. He didn't recognize him. He fired a shot into his head just to make sure the man was dead.

Hearing the slamming of car doors outside, he darted down the steps, hoping to catch the rest of the intruders before they escaped. By the time he opened the front door, they were already pulling off. That didn't stop him from letting off a few shots at the car, hoping to slow them enough that he could catch up. Snatching the keys to the Escalade off of the key hook, he ran out to the truck. His adrenalin was flowing so much, he never noticed or felt the bullet wounds that he'd suffered to his shoulder and left thigh, nor did they slow him down. Throwing the truck into Drive, he pulled recklessly from his driveway and gunned in the direction he last saw them travel.

"Yo, EZ! Load the gat up . . . I think this nigga coming. Hold up. Hold up. Get down real quick. Police headed toward his crib. Let them pass first. I hope ain't nobody get the description of this car," Leaf conveyed in obvious panic. They had to cross two more lights before getting back on the expressway to Philly. It seemed like the lights took forever to change. Leaf was watching the rearview mirror the entire time, while EZ reloaded the Glock. Once they made it on to the expressway, relief set it. But not for EZ. He started crying and talking some shit that didn't make any sense.

"We got to go back! We got to get Ikeal out of there. He might not have been dead. Come on, Leaf, turn this mafucka around, dog. Real talk," he ordered with the gun pointed to Leaf's side.

"Motherfucka, is you crazy? The nigga dead! Police gonna be all over that mafucka! Give me this fuckin' gun, nigga," he snapped before snatching the gun from his hand. While he was busy arguing with EZ, he momentarily was off guard. This prohibited him from observing the black Escalade that pulled up beside him with an AK hanging out of the window—until it was too late. Several shots came through the window. He was only grazed in the arm, but the impact caused him to lose control and swerve around dangerously. They sideswiped another car before miraculously regaining control. Once he glanced into the rearview mirror and discovered that Black was now a few cars behind him, he then turned his attention to EZ.

"See what the fuck your dumb ass made me do? You almost got me killed, nigga . . . You stupid motherfucka!" *Boop! Boop! Boop!* He shot him in the head three times at point-blank range. Numerous motorists pulled to the side of the road to let him pass. As he did, he observed some of them talking on their cell phones and staring at him in disbelief and fear. Realizing they were calling the police, he cracked his neck on both sides, preparing to finish off what he started. He slowed the car up significantly, allowing Black to catch up. From a distance, he spotted the blue and red flashing lights blocking the roads ahead of him. He managed to get on the blindside of the truck. While the speed started to pick back up, they slammed their cars into each other, trying to run each other off the road. The road block was just ahead of them, and their speed was well over 60 miles per hour, and picking up. The state troopers had no choice but to start firing. One of their bullets hit the tire of the Escalade, sending it slamming into the median before flipping over several times, eventually landing on its roof.

When police fire finally ceased, Leaf's car was inoperable. He jumped out and ran in the opposite direction. The troopers unleashed two full-grown fierce German shepherds that quickly caught up to him and began biting at his legs. He was able to get two shots off into one of the dogs before the other forcefully took him down to the ground.

Decisions and Drastic Measures

Adam made sure to get a written and signed certificate of agreement with Gus before transporting him out of the jail in an ambulance filled with federal agents. The agreement consisted of him pleading guilty to the crimes he was accused of, confessing to his criminal history and lifestyle, and fully cooperating with the United States Government. Gus had tried to get immunity for Trisha and his mom too, but they told him the girls would have to sign their own certificate of agreements. Failure to live up to his end of the agreement would result in his guilty plea being used against him. He would then be sentenced to the maximum term allowed. Part of him denied that he had agreed to such an arrangement. At this point, there was no sense in crying over spilled milk. It was now him against the world.

He was wheeled into the hospital and taken to ICU where his wife was being treated. Once the room was secure, they unlocked the shackles on his feet and helped him over to the side of her bed. He was still in a lot of pain himself, but after looking at his wife's bruised and battered body, his pain was numbed. Leaning over, he kissed her on the forehead while rubbing his hands softly over her body. Hoping that she could hear him, he begged her to hold on to life.

"Baby, you got to hold on. You're all I got left. I'm nothing without you. Fight, baby! If you make it out of this one, I promise you that I'm done with all that bullshit. I just want it to be me and you, that's it. I've already took the proper steps needed to get out of my situation, now I just need you to get out of yours. Squeeze my hand if you can hear me, baby," he encouraged while holding her right hand in his. At first, there was no reaction. But after a few moments, he felt a slight movement from her hand. Adam walked over and added his two cents to the situation.

"You already know who is responsible for this. If you don't stop him now, you'll never stop him. He surely won't stop until you and everything you love is dead. Think about it . . . Y'all are the only ones that can hurt him right now. After seeing for yourself that this man will stop at nothing to silence you, I hope for your sake that you stay true to your word and give us your full assistance."

All this was part of the strategy used to further influence Gus's cooperation. The hospital visit, the encouragement, and the pretend show—as though they really cared. In all actuality, it was just part of the job. When the feds wanted someone, they were persistent and exercised every remedy and resource they had to get the individuals off the street. Even if it meant they had to cut a deal with another criminal to get a bigger criminal off the streets, so be it. They wouldn't care if someone came forward and said they did some sort of criminal activities with the individuals years ago. If it was reliable and useful to the prosecution, they would have a 5K1 letter prepared to exchange for the information and testimony. Their methods of operation are proven to be extremely effective in the federal system. Regardless of what you are worth financially, who you had backing you, and what evidence they had against you, if you weren't working with them, your ass would be floating up shit creek.

When Connie regained consciousness, she stared around the room in wonder and confusion. She had little recollection of what took place to put her in the hospital, but the injuries were obvious. She lifted the shirt of the hospital scrubs she was wearing and studied the bandages on her lower side and back. She realized that they were entry and exit wounds. Feeling a burning, stinging sensation on her face, she patted across it with her hands, only to feel stitches and lacerations. Slowly but surely, she started remembering the night of the attempted assassination. More importantly, she remembered the gun and money that were in the trunk and could possibly be linked to her. She became instantly paranoid. Nothing else mattered to her at that moment but getting out of the hospital. As she was climbing out of the bed, a nurse walked in and tried to stop her.

"Miss, please lie back down. You were in a very serious accident last night, plus you were shot. We're still conducting tests on you. Trust me, you're in no condition to even be standing up," she advised.

"I appreciate your advice, but I'm a big girl, and I'm leaving this mafuckin' hospital right now. So, either you come over here and take these IVs out of my arm, or I'll do it myself."

"I'm going to let the doctor take care of this," she replied before stomping out of the room. By the time the doctor returned, she had already removed the IV, found her shoes, and was on her way out. The doctor really didn't care whether she stayed or left, but he was told by the detectives to contact them once she began improving. When the nurse informed him that she was attempting to leave, he contacted the detective who instructed him to hold her there as long as possible. In an attempt to do so, he asked her to sign papers.

"Ma'am, these are the release papers that you must sign before leaving. It just states that the hospital is not responsible or liable for anything that happens to you once you leave the premises. Plus, if you'll stay for a minute, I can write a few prescriptions for pain and infection."

"Sure, that would be nice. Just give me two minutes to step outside and smoke a cigarette. I'll be right back in," she gamed. After recognizing that the doctor was trying to delay her exit, her suspicions were raised, prompting her to get out of there even faster. It was very difficult for her to walk, but she somehow mustered enough energy to do it. While riding the elevator downstairs, she had flashbacks of the way Jihad's brains were savagely blown all over the place. She was actually falling in love with the nigga, so it was only right that she shed a few tears in his memory. There was no question that Black was behind the hit, because he was the only one that knew where they were eating. She promised to get down to the bottom of it once she got herself together.

As Connie stepped off the elevator, her heart damn near jumped out of her chest when she came face-to-face with a dozen state police. At first, she thought they were coming for her but quickly realized that they were bringing in a prisoner. As she turned to walk away, she thought she was hearing things when someone screamed her name with aggression.

"Get the fuck up off me. Let me go pig motherfuckers."

Connie would have sworn it was her nephew Leaf's voice. The voice was so close that she thought he was directly behind her. When she turned to take a look, she made eye to eye contact with her nephew. He looked pretty banged up, and the state troopers had him in cuffs and shackled to the wheelchair he was sitting in.

"Connie, you trifling-ass bitch! Did you kill my brother?" Leaf barked when he saw her. She decided it was in her best interest to ignore him and kept it moving. Her life had turned into a living nightmare. Things just weren't adding up. Everything was happening way too fast. Not having a clue where she was headed, she flew out of that hospital and put as much distance between it and her as she could.

Adam had just told Gus that he had about twenty minutes left before he had to be returned to jail when an informative call came from his fellow agent, Amy.

"I hope you're sitting down because when I bring you up to speed on what took place over the last twenty-four hours, you are going to think I am full of shit," she exclaimed. "Well, since we were both present last night, I'll move right along. A little after five this morning, Consuela Santana apparently staked out Black's wife's day care center. When Chyna arrived with her daughter, Consuela crept up and killed both of them."

"Are you fucking serious?" Adam interrupted.

"Yes . . . but wait, there's more. After the killings, she drove to the cemetery where her son was buried, placed a call, and then killed herself. But the best part is still yet to come. We believe that the call was placed to Ka'Leaf because he gathered his two goons from South Philly, and they made their way over to Black's King of Prussia residence. They forced their entry inside, killed the housekeeper, and began a deadly gun battle in which one of the South Philly guys was killed. The shoot-out some-how escalated to the expressway. After police received calls from a dozen motorists who witnessed it, they set up a road block on the expressway. When the state troopers realized that neither suspect had intentions of slowing down nor surrendering, they opened fire. Black ended up flipping his truck while Leaf tried to escape on foot. They let the dogs go on him, and, in turn, he shot one of them before the other mauled him down to the ground. Black suffered head and spinal injuries, but I am by his side making sure he pulls through. We're at Thomas Jefferson Hospital."

"Please tell me there's no more . . . I already got a serious fucking headache, Amy."

"Well, there is one last thing, but you're not going to believe it. I instructed the doctor over at the hospital to call me the second Connie opened her eyes, and that just happened to be around the time I was busy with this mess on the expressway. However, I told him to buy a little time so I could have someone go over and keep a close eye on her. But he let the bitch leave. While I was in the ambulance watching over Black, the crime lab is calling me like crazy, but this piece-of-shit Nextel phone isn't getting any reception. When I finally checked my messages, I got the surprise of a lifetime. They said the weapon we confiscated from out of the trunk of the BMW was the murder weapon used to kill Sha'Ron Santana. And, guess whose fingerprints and DNA were all over it?"

"Connie's? Wow! I need a minute, Amy. I'll call you as soon as I drop Gus back off at the Federal Detention Center. We have a very important meeting tomorrow over at the courthouse, and we all need to sit down and discuss these developments before that happens. Talk to you in a little."

Before dropping Gus off at the jail, Adam reminded him that he would see him the following day, and suggested he get a good sleep. Afterward, he rushed over to the other hospital to join Amy. When he arrived, he bumped into his fellow agents outside the trauma unit who were engaged in deep conversation with one of the doctors. He caught only a portion of the discussion.

"We appreciate all of your efforts, Doctor, but we need you to do everything in your power to ensure this patient survives. He has caused a lot of mischief on these streets and put numerous lives at stake. It would be a great service to the community and the United States Government if this man pulls through to face justice. We're aware that you're one of the best doctors here, and we are prepared to see to it that you'll get the full recognition, as well as compensation, from the U.S. Government if he pulls through," explained the agent.

This was another example showing how the feds would stop at nothing to get their man. They were masters at understanding the human mind. People who were promised something in return for their assistance were likely to put more effort into the task than someone who was not. The exchange policy was their most effective practice, out of all their resources. If the doctor was only giving the patient 40 percent of his effort before, he was now giving 100 percent. The doctor began working on the patient as if he were the closest of kin. Had he not given his best, the patient would likely have died from the injuries sustained.

Showtime . . . All for All!

The following morning, Gus was awakened at 4:00 a.m. and notified that he was scheduled for court. The officer advised him that he had thirty minutes to be showered, dressed, and ready to go. His body was still sore from the stabbings, not to mention the emotional pain he had knowing his wife was in such bad shape. Acknowledging the fact that he and his wife's survival was based on him making a deal with the feds, he swallowed his pride and focused on the big picture . . . which, by his perspective, meant getting out of jail by any means.

After being escorted downstairs to an overcrowded holding tank, he placed his back against the wall and put on the meanest face he could muster. The conversations he heard some of the other inmates discussing openly gave him a chilling realization of how serious the feds were. Some talked about how they had lost a trial because a close friend or family member testified on them, and now they were facing decades of incarceration. Some of their charges were similar to his, which made him a little nervous. Then, there were other inmates that boasted proudly of how they were cooperating with the feds to get reduced sentences. They made it sound as if it was morally correct and acceptable. Now, he understood what the rapper Jeezy meant about having federal nightmares . . . He was now in the middle of one.

Soon afterward, the federal marshals arrived to transport them over to the courthouse. He was placed in a cell that was used to hold the inmates scheduled to proffer (i.e., meet with the federal agents and give information). While waiting to be called, a male figure walking with crutches caught his attention. He couldn't believe his eyes. Once he had a second look, he was certain it was his cousin, Leaf. They made eye contact briefly before Leaf took the opportunity to whisper insults and threats, which Gus was able to lip-read.

"I'ma kill you and your mom, pussy. I know what y'all did." Gus didn't respond. Instead, he chose to ignore him. *What the fuck is Leaf talking about? What does he think we did now? And how the hell did he end up getting arrested? He must have just got locked up because he still has on street clothes,* he thought to himself. Soon after, the marshals came to the cell and called his name.

"Gus Santana! Come with us." They walked to a far corner of the building and stopped at an elevator. After the marshals pushed a sequence of codes into the security keypad, it allowed the elevator to come down. When the door opened, Amy and Adam were standing there with serious postures. After signing a few required forms, they were given custody of the prisoner.

Five minutes later, they were being seated inside Prosecutor Joe Khann's office. After inquiries and introductions were exchanged, they got right down to business. Joe held no punches getting right to the point.

"Fortunately for you, young man, you came to your senses and decided to do the right thing. I don't know if you are aware, but your cousin Ka'Leaf has been indicted on interstate murder, firearms violations, and killing a police officer. The cop-killing charge stemmed from him shooting a police K-9, which is practically the same as shooting an officer. We also have Black in custody as well. Unfortunately for Mr. Campbell, he has suffered serious injuries resulting from the incident involving your cousin Ka'Leaf Santana. He remains hospitalized, but we are hopeful that he'll pull through in a few weeks. The moment he starts improving, we're going to pull him over here and charge him with murder, drug trafficking, and conspiracy charges.

"As our agreement with you states, you are obligated to provide truthful and full details of your role in the drug conspiracy, as well as Black's status as your boss and supplier. Please understand that if anything else comes up that we feel requires your cooperation, you will have no choice in the matter . . . regardless if it's your mother, cousin, wife, boss, best friend, enemy, or associate. I hope I've made myself clear on that. If you renege on the deal, then so will we," he explained with a serious expression.

"Now that we have that squared away, let's move right along to what I need to get done today. I want you to give me a detailed version of how you met Black, your first drug transaction, an estimate of the amount of drugs he supplied you with, your relationship, and any associates you were introduced to through him, and anything else that may be essential toward our investigation. If I'm satisfied with what I hear, and I'm convinced that you are providing me with the official version, I'm going to grant you bail under your own recognizance. However, because of the nature of your crimes and your protection, you will be given minimum freedom until the case is over. Therefore, you will be under the twenty-four-hour supervision of a federal agent and kept at an undisclosed area. The only person other than us that will have access to the location is your wife. She will be taken there once she is stabilized. She'll be subjected to the same rules and regulations as you, and she has to sign her papers acknowledging that she is cooperating as well. I warn you, if either of you break the rules, you'll both be sent back to prison.

I will not jeopardize the lives of federal agents for carelessness or stupidity. Before I hear anything you have to say, I want you to verbally acknowledge that you understand, and then if you have any questions, now is the time to come forward with them," he advised.

Gus sat there speechless as he digested every word that Joe had said to him. There were so many things that made no sense, so many questions that he wanted answered but was afraid to ask. He had already been informed that Jihad was working for them ever since being released from jail. But what he didn't understand was how he witnessed with his own eyes Jihad shoot and possibly kill people while he was working for the feds. Did they excuse it? Permit it? Hide it, or what? *These mafuckas is Hollywood, for real. This shit like a chess match. What the fuck did I get myself into? I feel like a piece of shit. Please, somebody walk through the door and tell me this is a bad dream or another test. Fuck it. Reality of the matter is, this shit is definitely real. I got reason to cross these slimy niggas anyway. Ain't no turning back now. I can't kill my way out like the state system. I damn sure can't fight my way out, so fuck it. I'ma talk my way out of this shit,* he thought quietly while building himself up enough courage for the challenge ahead.

"Yes, I understand everything you said. As far as questions are concerned, I got millions of them, but I'd rather not know the answers. Trying to figure this shit out here is virtually impossible, so I'd rather avoid the headache and just go with the flow," he responded with an answer that made the agents and prosecutor slightly relieved.

It took him close to three hours to explain the incriminating details of his and Black's relationship on a personal level, as well as on a business level. He answered all questions honestly and exactly how the feds wanted him to. Through the story and the questioning, the feds discovered that he wasn't as dumb as they painted him out to be. He was actually intelligent and knew how to fulfill the position as he was expected to. In fact, the information he provided was so informative and reliable that the agents and prosecutor stared at one another with surprised expressions several times throughout his informing.

They smiled, laughed, sighed, and whistled while showing their overwhelming excitement. Before the meeting concluded, Joe thanked Gus and notified him that he would be freed from the jail later that evening. But, like all good news, it usually came with some bad. This time, Amy was chosen to deliver the bad news.

"With so much going on, this has really been our first chance to touch base on a few things. I want to start off by informing you that your aunt Consuela was found dead in Cobbscreek Cemetery by an apparent self-inflicted gunshot wound to the head. I'm sorry for being late to inform you of that, and my condolences go out to your loved ones.

"Next, we believe that the man who stabbed you and critically injured your cellmate was hired by Black. We believe the lawyer was responsible for arranging it while on an unmonitored legal visit the previous day. He will be charged with witness intimidation and arranging a contract killing, eventually. That matter is still being investigated.

"Last but not least, your mother was found to be in possession of a weapon . . . the same one that killed Sha'Ron. Murder charges are still pending in that case. As of yesterday, she slipped out of the hospital and has not been seen or heard from since." The only reason they hadn't relayed the message to him at the beginning of the meeting was because they didn't want the news to discourage him from cooperating, nor cloud his memory.

Gus showed no emotion. He simply registered the information and decided that once he got out of there, he would have time to focus on family and other issues. But for now, he had to do for himself. After the appropriate paperwork was signed and submitted, Gus was released into the custody of federal agents.

After Leaf was booked, processed, and fingerprinted, he was transported over to the Federal Detention Center. While being screened, he was informed that because of the nature of his charges, he was being placed in administrative segregation indefinitely. He was given an orange jumpsuit and placed in a cell by himself. While he waited for an officer to escort him to the hole, he spotted the marshals returning the inmates that went to court that day. When he didn't see Gus, he became suspicious. *Where the fuck this nigga at? I was hoping to bump heads so I could get at his bitch ass. I wonder if one of those marshals will tell me where he at.*

"Ay, Marshal! Why y'all ain't bring my cousin back over? Gus Santana. He went to court earlier today and ain't came back yet," he screamed at the marshal through the side of the door. The marshal looked at a piece of paper he held in his hand before responding.

"He bailed out today, my man."

Leaf was overcome with hatred and jealousy as a result of those findings. *How the fuck this nigga always getting out of something? That bitch-ass nigga must got a rabbit foot up his ass. I can't stand that nigga. I got to get the fuck up out of here*, he reasoned with himself. Twenty minutes later, he was escorted up to the hole. While en route to his cell, they passed dozens of other cells. Some of the inmates gave him mean stares, while others banged on their doors and screamed insults or threats. Once he stepped into the cell, the door was secured. He stood there staring around at his small cell, trying his hardest to adapt to the new environment, and possibly his final home.

Now that he was alone, he had time to reflect on his life. He thought about his brother, the separation of his family, his South Philly homies, Nicki, and most importantly, his mother. He thought about the last conversation he had with her and how odd it seemed. He was worried out of his mind for her. With everything he was going through, it finally got the best of him. For just that night, he separated himself from the gangsta image he portrayed and lived by. Only then did he lie in his bed and cry himself to sleep.

The Greatest Trick
the Devil Pulled?

Fooling the World
He Didn't Exist

Over the course of the next few weeks, there were several new developments in the drug conspiracy involving Black and the Santanas. Ryan McMonagle was not only representing Black, but he had also appointed a private doctor to tend to his injuries. Allegedly, Black had developed a severe case of amnesia ever since coming out of his coma and was supposedly unresponsive to communication. His condition was similar to a person in a vegetative state. In addition to his injuries, he also suffered from paralysis as a result of the spinal fracture. McMonagle had filed numerous motions to keep him out of prison and in the hospital, which were granted with stipulations. He was under twenty-four-hour guard, and no visitors except attorney and doctors were allowed. The feds weren't buying any of his claims. In fact, they were still aggressively proceeding with preparation for the trial. At a plea hearing on Black's behalf, McMonagle entered a plea of not guilty, stating that his client's mental and medical condition made him incompetent to stand trial.

The anticipated trial was set to begin in three weeks. The case against Black mainly rested on Gus's testimony. The other incident involving him and Leaf could be justified as self-defense because they invaded his home and initiated the gun battle. Coincidentally, the two were now codefendants. With or without Gus's testimony, Leaf was finished. They had linked him to several homicides throughout the city, including that of his girlfriend, Nicki. The evidence against him was overwhelming, so their main concern was obtaining a conviction against Black. Federal prosecutors and agents visited Gus for hours on a daily basis and prepped him intensely for the trial. Their intentions were to continue to prep him all the way to the day of the trial.

B.O.R.E.—Bitch on the Run Eating

Trying to reestablish herself while on the run proved to be difficult for Connie. The feds were persistently trying to capture her. It seemed like everywhere she went, they caught wind of it and swarmed the place. In some instances, she had only escaped them by mere seconds. Eventually, she was able to find refuge in Willingboro, New Jersey, with her friend, Drea, whom she had done time with in the feds. Drea had the town on lockdown, and Connie was able to put her on an out-of-town connection that supplied good coke at a better price than she was getting . . . And on the strength that, her connection had no problem fronting a large amount of work. In an exchange for the new line, Drea made Connie her partner. Being a veteran hustler, Connie was able to show Drea the ropes and shortcuts to get rich fast. The money was pouring in. Connie had changed her appearance dramatically. She cut all her hair off and dyed it blond. She always wore dark glasses and never traveled unless it was with a licensed driver. To help her cope with her personal family issues, she started to drink obsessively. That and getting money were the only things that allowed her to escape the reality of the fact that she killed her nephew (the wrong one), which led to her sister killing herself. Her son had destroyed the Santana name by ratting. For that, she could never forgive him. She was now on the run from the feds. She knew that it was only a matter of time before they would catch up to her, and she was prepared to declare court on the streets.

Ever since discovering through the newspaper that Jihad was a rat working for the feds, she refused to involve herself with any other men. They were not to be trusted. Her body felt violated and abused to the same degree as a rape victim. Through newspapers, she also stayed posted on Black's situation and the claims his lawyer and doctors were making. Her feelings concerning him were extremely malicious. At night, she had difficulty sleeping, knowing that he was still breathing. She couldn't let him get away with turning against them and almost getting her son killed. Even though she was beyond pissed at her son for ratting, she wasn't willing to let anybody hurt him. The only person that could ever take him out was herself. She desperately wanted to make Black suffer the most painful death imaginable. And that motherfucking lawyer Ryan had something coming for him too. Had the opportunity presented itself, she would be delighted to carry out her wishes.

Stand Up, Nigga!

Over the last few weeks of incarceration, Leaf had adapted to his habitat very well. He had two next-door neighbors who "went hard" (weren't snitching and were fighting the U.S. Government) and had no problem showing their paperwork to prove it. Once they all discovered they shared the same principles and morals, they got tight and started conversing through the wall. Their names were Shabazz and Shyst. At first, Shabazz thought he was going to have a problem with Leaf because of what he had done to his family, but when Shabazz heard him speak about Gus, the hatred and disassociation was obvious. He would call him a rat, faggot, and other insults. They constantly spoke about their regrets of not killing him. But Leaf was more disappointed in Shabazz because he had gotten close enough to do it but couldn't finish the job.

Leaf was unaware of any and everything that took place since he was locked up. Not one person had contacted him to inform him of anything, nor did he receive any form of correspondence. He'd been wondering why his mom hadn't gotten in contact with him yet. He tried calling her once when they let him use a phone, but her phone went straight to voice mail. It was as if everyone had gone ghost on him. With the exception of his arraignment, he hadn't even seen his court-appointed attorney yet. The system was trying to railroad him by all means.

One evening, he received his discovery (legal details surrounding a case), and it uncovered some disturbing news. The beginning of the discovery stated how the feds had employed Jihad to infiltrate the family business. Wearing a wire and reporting additional information, they were able to build mountains of evidence against them. As he continued to read, he found out that Jihad was killed, and Gus was ratting, just as suspected. He set the paperwork down so that he could share this new information with his two neighbors.

"Ay, Shyst! Shabazz! Y'all niggas ain't gonna believe this. I got my case papers today, and don't you know this bitch-ass nigga from my hood that used to put that work in was working for the fucking feds the entire time. Somebody killed that faggot a few weeks back. What's crazy about that is, the nigga was still busting his gun and acting like he was a fucking gangsta. Rat-ass nigga. Then Gus. This nigga was out there doing him, getting money, and pushing that work like it was no tomorrow. When shit got rough, he want to take the easy way out. Niggas don't just turn to rats overnight; them niggas was born rats. The FBI need to turn their name to the SPCA because that's all they do is pick up the snakes, rats, and a couple of us cats and dogs. This shit got me mad as a motherfucker, and I'm only halfway through it. I'ma finish reading this shit in a few minutes. What's up with y'all niggas?"

"Ain't shit. I'm over here getting a crazy workout, you heard," chimed Shyst with his New York accent.

"Man, I'm over here reading that *Thugs and Gangstas* by the nigga, Ross. That's fucked up that you had to find out about the niggas you used to fuck with now that it's too late to take action. But you know them rats will never be comfortable or successful. They gave up their

names and their honor to get out of something they knew
was possible to happen while living that lifestyle. They
would never look in the mirror and be satisfied with their
reflection. Real talk! Go ahead and finish reading your
legal work, but feel relieved knowing that your name,
reputation, and legend will live forever, regardless of the
outcome. That alone will give you a richness of heart that
you can cash in on at any given time," preached Shabazz.

Though Leaf didn't respond, the words penetrated
his heart and mind and were deeply felt. As he continued his reading, he came across Connie's warrant,
issued for the possession of a firearm by a convicted
felon and for the murder of Sha'Ron. Once he saw it
confirmed in writing, it made him feel even worse. Had
he just listened to Nicki, the events that led up to his
arrest would never have taken place. He felt like shit for
killing her, and it made him hate his aunt Connie even
more. Knowing that she was still on the run only made
him more furious with himself. Not wanting to dwell
on it any longer, he continued to move along. On the
very next page, he came across news that was so sickening that everything in his stomach vomited up violently. He then fell to the floor, crying hysterically. After
a few minutes, he crawled over to the door and began
punching it with his fist, as hard as he could. He ignored
all pleas from his two neighbors to stop and explain
what was going on. By the time the responding officers
subdued him by using Mace and rubber bullets, both
his hands were broken and covered in blood. As they
dragged him to the infirmary for medical attention, he
wept repeatedly.

"Mommy! Mommy!" The few threads that kept him
together after the death of his brother were no longer
of any use. In fact, all the stitches in the world couldn't
sew his heart back together again. He had reached his

breaking point. The physical and mental anguish that he suffered from would lead to him being evaluated as a person who developed a severe psychopathic disorder. This illness would eventually persuade him to plea out to multiple life sentences, taking the fight out of him. Insanity was an understatement.

Where I Need to Be

Ever since Trish had gotten out of the hospital, Gus had been showering her with affection. He was extradelicate while touching her and during lovemaking. He constantly expressed how grateful he was to still have her, and how sorry he was that she almost lost her life due to his dangerous lifestyle. She accepted his apologies because she believed that everything he was doing was to put the past life behind and move on with their new life. Gus still had a lot of obligations to fulfill for the government before he could realistically start planning ahead. The beginning of the trial was just a week away, and his performance would dictate his freedom. He intended to cover his part to the fullest.

The feds made him aware that they possibly would use him in another trial, if the investigation led to charges being filed against Ryan McMonagle for witness intimidation and murder for hire. Gus was willing to do whatever he needed to do in order to maintain his freedom.

Kalid had survived his injuries and was back in his cell. For his troubles, the feds did follow through and get him his Quran. He also got some time shaved off his sentence and was due to be released in two years. Kalid was still willing to assist the feds in any way possible.

Time Has Come

The most anticipated trial of the year started on the first day of summer. The weather was mild and muggy. As expected, over a hundred people showed up to observe the trial. Most were supporters for Black, and others came just to witness a member of the legendary Santana family go against the codes of the street. The courtroom was so packed that there were closed circuit televisions set up in the hallway and in other courtrooms.

When the U.S. Marshals pushed Black's wheelchair through the courtroom, those in attendance were shocked at what they saw. The man that they once acknowledged as a boss appeared as if he was in great distress. His hair was unkempt, as was his beard. He had lost a remarkable amount of weight, and his face was emotionless. Some of the people made comments out loud concerning how he looked, prompting the judge to bang his gavel to restore order.

Opening arguments soon began, where the opposing lawyers fiercely battled for the jurors' favor. Ryan produced several witnesses, such as doctors, psychiatrists, and other specialists. They all testified that Black suffered from post-traumatic stress syndrome, and that he had experienced a severe memory loss with no recollection of his past life. In response, Joe produced doctors that were employed by the government to challenge and dispute the claims. It was up to the jurors to decide whose testimony was more convincing. Most of the afternoon was spent listening to incriminating wiretap conversations between

Black and Gus. There was discussions ranging from murder to extortion, drug dealing to legitimate business. The way Black gave orders over the wiretap, it was clear to see that he was the shot caller of the organization, as well as a close associate to the star witness, scheduled to testify the following afternoon.

The next day, when Gus entered the courtroom, he was escorted by two federal agents who walked him up to the witness stand. He wore a sharp navy blue business suit, complemented by a pair of eyeglasses which gave him a professional look. After being sworn in, he set out to earn the government's favor. His testimony was impeccable. Even while under an aggressive cross-examination by Black's lawyer, he held his ground. His testimony was credible and extremely damaging to the defense, which made the feds very grateful.

During closing arguments, Black's lawyer had one final stunt in an attempt to secure a not-guilty verdict. He pushed Black's wheelchair directly in front of the jury, then instructed them to stare Black in his eyes.

"Tell me, is achieving justice possible in this case? Look at this man. He has the mental capacity of a two-year-old boy. He has to be fed, dressed, washed, changed, and watched twenty-four hours a day. Prison doesn't provide those services. More importantly, he has no recollection of any of these things which he's accused of. The law clearly states that a person must understand what he is being charged with, as well as the punishment that is being rendered against him. This man can't count to one, let alone understand what's happening right now. Even if you examine the evidence closely, this case is nothing but mere hearsay from a bunch of criminals who entrapped my client, as the government alleges, conspired with my client, and then cut deals with the U.S. Government to save their own tails by going against my client.

"Did you hear the testimony of Gus Santana? Was it not the most perfectly rehearsed speech you've ever heard? Even I couldn't catch him in a lie or get him to twist his story up, and that's mighty rare. I hope that you, the people of the jury, do not allow a great injustice to take place on your watch. I thank you for your time and undivided attention," he concluded before pushing Black's wheelchair back over to the side of the defense table. His closing left a hell of an impression on the jury, leaving them in deep thought as Joe prepared to give his closing.

As the seasoned prosecutor approached the jury, he stared each one of them up and down, while walking down the aisle in front of them. He then started clapping his hands sarcastically.

"Talk about performance. That closing deserves a nomination for an Oscar."

"I object, Your Honor," Black's lawyer yelled.

"Strike that, Your Honor. I apologize. That's what a man does, people. He takes responsibility for his actions. Right is right, and wrong is wrong. Every citizen of the United States that commits a crime must be held responsible and punished according to the statute of the law. If not, we have no civilization. People would cause mischief beyond repair throughout the land. You, the people of the jury, have a duty to uphold the law. Please, do not be deceived by these fabricated pictures painted by the defense. Know that every picture tells a thousand stories. I look forward to you, the jury, assisting this country in ridding our communities of urban terrorists such as this man, Curtis Campbell," he spat while pointing at Black vigorously.

After the judge sent the jury into the chambers to deliberate, he ordered a recess in the court. The people in attendance were very curious and interested to see the verdict the jury would deliver.

After two days of deliberation, the jury had finally reached a verdict. The crowd of observers seemed to have doubled, as people flooded in and around the courtroom to witness the verdict for themselves. It was common practice for the judge to question the foreman concerning the verdict.

"Foreman, have you the jury reached a verdict?"

"We have, Your Honor. In the case of United States versus Greg Hutton, we, the jury, find the defendant not guilty of all charges!" The people in the courtroom went into a frenzy. The presiding judge banged his gavel several times to restore order. Once order was reestablished, he addressed Black's lawyer, and strongly advised him on what should be the next step for his client.

"Counsel, I strongly recommend that you immediately check this man into a mental institution, where he could get the proper treatment necessary for him to rehabilitate his mind and have a chance to recover. Nothing further. He's free to go."

"Thanks for the advice, Your Honor. But you see, Mr. Campbell is not just my client but also a personal friend of mine. He's in great hands," the lawyer explained. As he pushed Black out of the courtroom, they passed by the federal prosecutors and agents that built the case. Not only did Black smile at them, but he also winked and slightly smirked. That drove them furious. As Black and his attorney exited the courthouse, they were approached by several media outlets that bombarded McMonagle with a host of questions.

"How does it feel, securing yet another victory in federal court?"

"Where does your client go from here?"

"Did your client fake injuries to escape justice?"

As the lawyer stopped to answer the questions, Black took notice of a set of familiar eyes that were partially hidden underneath a female Muslim garb. The intent in her eyes was obvious, and all he could do was brace himself for the attack. A dozen or so shots rang off, sending the crowd into a panic—all with the exception of two whose bodies were stretched out across the path of the courthouse.

Joe, Adam, and Amy were discussing their disappointments and lost trust in the justice system when they heard the shots sound off. Believing that it was somehow connected to Black, they sprang out of the courtroom in the direction of the shooting. They came upon the two bodies. Black's lawyer lay dead on the ground, while Black struggled to breathe. He stared at them with fear written all over his face and started to beg for help.

"Please . . . help me . . . help . . . me!" he pleaded weakly. When Amy pulled out her phone intending to call for help, her fellow colleagues stared at her as if she were crazy.

"Wait a minute . . . It's a miracle. He can speak again," Joe chimed sarcastically.

"Too bad my Nextel phone won't get any service . . . Damn phone," Amy reported.

"Someone call an ambulance," Joe requested in a whisper.

They all stared at each other and produced slight smiles. Remembering what he did to them, they winked back at him as he lay there dying a slow, painful death.

Epilogue

A few weeks after the trial, Gus and Trish were officially enlisted into the Federal Witness Protection Program. They were relocated to Palm Springs, California, and given new identities, a home, and even had a nice percentage of money and assets that had been seized from them, returned. After a year or so, however, they got bored with their new lifestyle.

They missed the action, respect, and status that came along with their past activities. They soon returned to their past lifestyle, but not before getting clearance from their federal employers. They're believed to have infiltrated numerous networks on the West Coast, bringing down hundreds in their wake. They may be coming to a city near you soon. Watch out.

Connie is still on the run. She's believed to have gotten in touch with her Spanish side, and is using her charm, wit, and beauty to frequently come and go across the Mexican border. She's been spotted all over the West Coast, but each time authorities get close, she vanishes.

Leaf is being housed at a federal facility in Butler, North Carolina, for people with serious mental issues. His condition continues to go downhill. He rarely showers, his appearance is frightening, and he constantly talks to himself about killing Connie and Gus. At night, he calls out to his mother, brother, and Nicki before crying himself to sleep.

The number of federal inmates cooperating has soared drastically over the last year. Everybody's snitching. Deals are secured daily that make Wall Street look like a telemarketing service. Knowing this, one must ask themselves . . . Is it worth the money?